"Let's get this injury seen to, and then you can have some hot breakfast."

Their gazes met for seconds. Her whiskey-brown eyes caused the oddest sensation in the pit of his stomach, like butterflies flittering from flower to flower.

Men's stomachs weren't supposed to flutter.

"Don't worry. I'm not going to hurt you." She smiled. Her eyes sparkled.

"Now take your pills and drink your coffee. I'll see you in the kitchen in ten minutes."

"Wait!" Isaac didn't know why he'd called out to her, and then realized he didn't want her to leave. It had been a long time since he'd had a conversation with anyone, much less a kindhearted woman who made him feel alive. "What's your name?"

"Margaret, but everyone calls me Molly," she said, whirled round and then was gone.

The door shut behind her and he stared at the spot where she'd stood. When she'd left, all the life seemed to have been sucked out of the tiny room with her.

Cheryl Williford and her veteran husband, Henry, live in South Texas, where they've raised three children, numerous foster children, alongside a menagerie of rescued cats, dogs and hamsters. Her love for writing began in a literature class and now her characters keep her grabbing for paper and pen. She is a member of her local ACFW and CWA chapters, and is a seamstress, watercolorist and loving grandmother. Her website is cherylwilliford.com.

Books by Cheryl Williford

Love Inspired

The Amish Widow's Secret
The Amish Midwife's Courtship

The Amish Midwife's Courtship

Cheryl Williford

HARLEQUIN® LOVE INSPIRED®

LOVE INSPIRED BOOKS

Recycling programs
for this product may
not exist in your area.

ISBN-13: 978-0-373-81913-3

The Amish Midwife's Courtship

Copyright © 2016 by Cheryl Williford

The Lord is good and does what is right; he shows
the proper path to those who go astray.
—*Psalms* 25:8

This book is dedicated to my husband, Henry, who's always there when I need him, and to Clare Naomi, our youngest granddaughter. Your smile makes the sun shine brighter. Much thanks goes to Barbara Burns and Susan Cobb, my daughters and two of my biggest fans, and to ACFW's Golden Girls critique group. Without you ladies I'd still be editing my own weak verbs.

Chapter One

❧

Pinecraft, Florida
November

Molly Ziegler gave the dust mop one last shove under the bed and hit a mahogany leg. Unexpected movement under the bed's mound of sheets and wedding-ring quilt caught her unaware.

She froze.

Something swung toward her head. Instinctively she launched the mop high into the air, warding off the coming blow.

The mop's handle connected with something solid.

A satisfying *clunk* rang out in her *mamm*'s tiny rental room. Her heart thumped in her chest as she stepped back from the bed, lost her balance and hit the floor. Her feet tangled in the folds of her skirt as she pushed away.

His dark brown hair wild from sleep, a gaunt-faced, broad-shouldered man gazed down at her, his dark green eyes wide with surprise. He dropped the wooden crutch he'd been holding. "Who are you?" His hand gingerly touched the bump on his forehead. His eyes narrowed in a wince.

The bump on his forehead grew and began to ooze blood.

He wasn't supposed to be in the bedroom at this time of the day. The door hadn't been locked.

In a stupor of surprise, she blinked. She had no brothers, and with the exception of her father who had passed away in his sleep five years earlier, she'd never seen a man in his nightclothes. There were dark shadows under his eyes. Thick stubble on his chin and upper lip told her she was dealing with an unmarried man.

Annoyed by his words, she scowled. "I was about to ask you the same thing. Cover yourself. There's a woman in your midst. You might be visiting Pinecraft, where rules are often bent and broken, but my *mamm*'s dress code is very strict and must be followed by all renters."

"It wonders me why you're showing off those lovely stockings to a man if your *mamm*'s dress code is so strict."

Molly's face burned as she swiftly straightened her skirt. She clambered to her feet, an already sour mood making her wish she stood taller than five foot nothing in her stocking feet.

She controlled the urge to stomp as she stepped away from the bed with all the dignity she could muster. Her hands brushed down the skirt of her plain Amish dress and cleaning apron. With eyes narrowed, she sliced the man with an icy glare. "My *mamm* and I run a decent boarding *haus*. Our ways are Plain, but we keep high standards."

"Anyone ever tell you that you're a bit grumpy in the morning?"

Molly tried to ignore the man's uncalled-for comment and smirk, even though she knew he was right. She had woken up grumpy, her sleep cut short by Frieda Lapp's early-morning call and delivery of a beautiful baby girl, who they planned to call Rachel after John's recently departed mother.

She inched toward the closed bedroom door. Her *mamm*'s rule was firm and told to every renter who stayed in their boardinghouse. "This room was to be vacated by noon. It's now past one. Didn't you see the sign when you paid your deposit?"

"I saw the sign, but I made other arrangements with Mrs. Ziegler late last night. I'll be staying for several days, perhaps a month until I can find a permanent place, now that I've bought the bike shop. Didn't she tell you?"

A thick line of blood trickled down the man's forehead, threatening to drip on the bed linens.

He must be Isaac Graber, the stay-over Mamm mentioned this morning, and now I've struck him.

She turned on her heel and shoved back the plain white curtains blowing at the window. A crutch lay by her foot. She found an identical crutch leaning against the bedpost.

Molly dug into her apron pocket and pulled out a clean tissue and thrust it into his hand. "Here. You need this. *Mamm* won't want blood on the sheets."

He pressed the tissue against the bump, then gazed down at the blot of scarlet blood. "You cut my head!" His coloring turned from primrose to a sickly mossy green.

"I wouldn't have hit you if you hadn't taken that swing at me with the crutch." She leaned in to hand him a wastebasket and then stepped back fast, inching her way toward the closed bedroom door. The man behaved like a brute, but she had to admit he was an attractive one. She'd never seen eyes so green and sparkling.

And such thick, glossy nut-brown hair. Dark strands jutted at every angle in the most unusual way.

Molly realized he was talking, and she tried to drag her attention away from his face and back to his words.

"I was asleep and you startled me awake. You could have been a thief, for all I knew."

"A thief!" She sucked in her breath and then chuckled. "That's rich. I was doing my job and *you* attacked me."

He kept talking as if she hadn't spoken. "I grabbed the closest thing I had to defend myself." He looked at the plastic trash can she'd placed on the edge of the mattress and gazed at her, befuddled, his forehead creasing. "What's this for?" he asked, swallowing hard.

"In case you vomit. Some people do when they see blood and turn that particular shade of green."

"Green? I'm not green. It's more likely I'm red from all the blood." He offered her the can, leaving his bloody fingerprints on the rim. "Take this thing away. I don't need it."

If Mamm *hears about all this, she'll rant*

for hours. Her eyes glanced at the small alarm clock on the bedside table and was shocked to see that time had gotten away from her. It was almost two. *I'll be late for singing rehearsal if I don't hurry.*

She snatched the can, her gaze on the impressive bump growing on the man's forehead. The cut was at least a half-inch long, blue as the sky and still dripping blood. "Does it hurt?" Her anger cooled and she began to feel contrite. "Maybe you could use some ice…a cloth?" She spoke softer "Maybe a doctor?"

He looked heavenward, rolling his eyes like a petulant teenager. "Oh, *now* the woman shows concern, and here I am thinking her a heartless thief." He pulled the sheet up and covered his thin sleeping shirt in mock alarm.

"Think what you will. Men usually do. Now, do you want a damp cloth or not, because I'm busy and don't have time for this foolishness."

"A cloth would be good if you're not too busy."

His sarcasm didn't go unnoticed. Her bad mood darkened. She grumbled to herself as she went into the old-fashioned, minuscule bathroom just off the bedroom. She didn't resent being told to clean the sparsely furnished back bedrooms when their last two renters left, but she'd already had her day planned.

She was used to hard work during their peak winter season, but holding down a job at the local café as a waitress and birthing babies as the local midwife kept her busy. Sometimes too busy. She liked the whirl of her demanding life, but she did resent her *mamm*'s attitude. Just because she was still single didn't mean she didn't have anything better to do on her day off than mop floors and strip down beds. She'd miss singing practice again this afternoon thanks to her *mamm*'s unreasonable demands on her time.

Her lip curled in an angry snarl as she pushed back a wayward strand of hair behind her ear, then ran a clean washcloth under cold running water.

Lifting her head, she caught a glimpse of herself in the mirror and scowled. Dishwater blonde hair that had been neatly pulled back in a tight bun now ran riot around her head. Remembering the renter's good looks, her cheeks flushed pink. What must he think of her appearance?

Her brown eyes flashing with frustration, she looked away, reprimanding herself for behaving like the frustrated twenty-year-old spinster she was.

With a jerk, she tugged her prayer *kapp* back into place and then squeezed the water out of the cloth. She was in enough trouble for hitting the man. Now wasn't the time to start ogling the guests and worrying about how she looked. The sin of vanity brought only strife into the life of a Plain person. She had to pull herself together.

The worn but well-polished hardwood floor squeaked as she hurried back to the bedroom and handed the cloth to the man. Their hands touched and she pulled away, not about to admit she felt anything.

But she had.

He ran his fingers through the dark spikes on his head and brought a semblance of order to his wild hair before wiping at the cut above his eyebrow.

"Here, let me do that. All you're doing is making it bleed again." Forgetting her own stringent proprieties, Molly moved to the bed, pulled her full skirt under her and sat as far away from him as she could and still touch him. She jerked the cloth from his fingers before he could object and dabbed lightly around the seeping wound.

"A butterfly bandage should take care of any further bleeding and keep the wound from scarring," she said. "The bandages and antibiotic cream are in the kitchen. I'll be right back."

She ran for the door, then skidded to a halt. "While I'm gone, please get out of bed and put on proper clothing." She bounded away, her skirt swirling around her legs as she hopped over the trash can and slipped out, letting the bedroom door bang behind her.

Isaac Graber's head hurt. He wiped the sticky blood off his fingers with the damp cloth the petite blonde-haired housekeeper had left behind and found himself smiling, something he hadn't done since the accident and his painful recovery.

The tiny woman had put him through sheer misery trying to keep up with her rapid-fire conversation. She taxed his patience and his temper, but he couldn't wait for her to come back into the room.

With a tug, he threw back the tangled covers and slid out of bed. The same white-hot agony that kept him up most nights stabbed down his leg. Angry red lines of surgical stitching laced up the puckered skin near his left knee and calf, his leg pale where the cast had covered it for several months.

He struggled to get into a pair of clean but well-worn trousers and a wrinkled long-sleeved cotton shirt he'd pulled from his suitcase, and then put on a fresh pair of socks and his scuffed boots, as he tried to forget the fresh ache in his head.

He'd taken his last pain medicine in Missouri, weeks before, and now had nothing to dull the ache in his leg or his heart. Not that he deserved the mind-numbing pills that helped him forget what he'd done and the tragedy he had rained down on his best friend's family.

Isaac dropped his chin to his chest and forced himself to breath slowly. He shouldn't have been driving that day, especially since the country road was slick after a sudden hard rain. He had no license. No insurance. Someone else could have taken Thomas home from the multi-church frolic when he'd wrenched his ankle. Why had he offered to drive? It wasn't like him to break Amish laws, even if Thomas's ankle was swollen after the rough game of volleyball.

With his eyes squeezed shut, his mind went back to the horrific day. The memory of Thomas lying on the ground next to him was seared in his mind.

The first police officer at the scene had assumed Thomas, who was Mennonite, had been driving. In shock and bleeding profusely, Isaac had been too confused to speak. He'd been rushed to the hospital and then into surgery.

But days later, when his thoughts had cleared, he'd heard the police were blaming the dead-drunk man in the other vehicle for the accident. Isaac knew they were wrong. Surely he was the one at fault and needed to make it right.

In the hospital, Isaac had confessed everything that day to his *daed*, but his father had railed at him, "We are Amish and will manage our own problems. You are to ask *Gott* for forgiveness and then be silent. I will not have the truth known to this community just to make you feel less guilty. Nothing can be gained by your confession. It was *Gott*'s will that Thomas die. You are to keep all this to yourself, do you hear, Isaac? You must tell no one. The shame you carry is yours, and yours alone. It is *Gott*'s punishment. You must learn to live with it. Your *mamm* and I will not be held up to ridicule because of your foolish choices. This kind of shame could kill your *mamm*. You know her heart is weak."

And like the coward he was, he'd run to Pinecraft, desperate to get away from his *daed*'s angry words, his mother's looks of shame. Isaac would spend the rest of his life dealing with things he could not change.

His hands braced against his legs, he looked down at his scuffed brown boots, at the crutch at his feet. He deserved to be crippled. If the police in Pinecraft ever found out the truth, he knew he'd be arrested, thrown into an *Englischer* jail for the rest of his life.

He rubbed the taunt muscle cramping in his leg. *Gott* was right to punish him for his foolish choices.

He smoothed down his trouser leg, covering the scar. Fatigue overwhelmed him. His guilt robbed him of sleep. He and Thomas had both died that day, but he knew he had to go on living.

A ridge of stitched skin under the trouser leg sent pain burning into his calf. No more *Englischer* doctors for him. All they wanted was to make him whole again. He didn't deserve to be free of pain. The doctors in Missouri should have let him die.

He'd have to find a way to deal with the ache in his heart, his guilt and the odd way he was forced to walk. Let people stare. He didn't care anymore. Nothing mattered. Thomas was dead.

The housemaid came swinging back into the

room with a tray of bandages, a bottle of aspirin and bowl of water. A steaming mug of black coffee sat in the middle of her clutter.

"I thought you might want something for the pain in your head." She set the tray on the nightstand, ruined his coffee with three packets of sugar and used a plastic spoon to stir it. With the twist of her delicate wrist, she unscrewed the aspirin bottle. "One or two?"

"None, *danke*," he said, and watched her count out two pills and place them on the table next to the coffee mug.

"Let's get this injury seen to and then you can have some hot breakfast. I put the biscuits back in the oven to warm. The last of the renters ate their meal at seven, but I'll make an exception for you this morning." She squeezed out the white washcloth floating in warm water and approached him, her pale eyebrows low with concentration.

Their gaze met for seconds. Her whiskey-brown eyes caused the oddest sensation in the pit of his stomach, like butterflies flittering from flower to flower. He frowned and hardened his resolve. The last thing he needed was a woman trying to take care of him.

"Don't worry. I'm not going to hurt you." She smiled. Her brown eyes sparkled.

He looked away, concentrating on the colorful braided rug on the floor. Her touch was gentle, the cream she spread with her fingertips cool and soothing. She unwrapped a small butterfly bandage and pressed it down, careful not to touch his cut.

"There, all done."

Tray in hand, she backed toward the door. "Now take your pills and drink your coffee. I'll see you in the kitchen in ten minutes."

"Wait!" He realized he didn't want her to leave. It had been a long time since he'd had a conversation with anyone, much less a kindhearted woman who made him feel alive. "What's your name?"

"Margaret, but everyone calls me Molly," she said, whirled round, and then was gone.

The door shut behind her, and he stared at the spot where she'd stood. When she left, all the life seemed to have been sucked out of the tiny room.

Molly leaned against the closed bedroom door and allowed herself to take a deep breath. She exhaled with a whoosh, then hurried back toward the kitchen. No man had ever affected her the way Isaac Graber did. She lifted her hand and watched it tremble. He had flustered her, made her pulse race. She was as happy as a *kinner* on Christmas morning and had no idea why.

Ridiculous! A man was already considering her for courtship, not that she was interested in him or ready for marriage to anyone. Still, her future had been mapped out by her *mamm*, and she really didn't have any choice in the matter.

No doubt she'd soon see the flaws in Isaac, like she did most men. She had to be practical. *Mamm* was counting on her to make a good marriage that would end all their financial problems.

She hurried through the hall and into the warm, cozy kitchen fragrant with the aroma of hot biscuits and sliced honey ham. At the stove, she turned on the gas, lit a blaze under the old iron frying pan and then added a spoon of reserved bacon fat.

Her hands still shook as she broke three eggs into a bowl and poured them into the hot oil. Crackling and popping, the eggs fried but were forgotten when the troublesome renter awkwardly maneuvered his way through the kitchen door, lost his balance and tripped over his own feet. He lay sprawled on the worn tile floor. Facedown. Not moving.

"Herr Graber!" Molly stepped over his crutch

and kneeled at his side. The morning headlines flashed through her mind. Man Killed by Abusive Landlady. "Please be all right." She shook his shoulder.

Nothing.

She shook it again, harder this time.

"If you'd stop trying to break my shoulder, I might be able to get up."

Molly stamped her foot, angrier than she'd been since he'd called her a thief earlier. Why did this man bring out the worst in her? "You scared me. Why didn't you say something, let me know you weren't dead? I thought…"

He leaned up on one elbow. "Did you seriously think I was dead? It would take a lot more than a spill to kill me, Miss Ziegler."

She gathered her skirt around her and scooted away, not sure what kind of mood he was in, but stayed close enough, just in case he needed help getting back on his feet.

His green eyes darted her way and then over to his fallen crutches. "Your mother seemed normal enough when I signed in last night. I wonder if she knows how you treat her guests when she's not around."

"I take offense to that remark, Herr Graber. I in no way harmed you. Well…here in the kitchen I didn't. I was busy cooking your

breakfast, and you fell over your own big feet."
He wore scarred, laced-up boots, the kind bikers favored. Maybe that was how he'd hurt himself. A nasty bike spill, and now he was in pain and taking his misery out on her.

"You're right. I did fall over my own feet. That's what cripples do." He leaned heavily on a single crutch and pushed his way to his feet, his face contorting with pain.

"*Ach*, you're no cripple," she said, standing.

"What would you know about being crippled?"

He'd crossed the line. Molly lifted her skirt an inch and showed him the built-up shoe on her right foot. "I think I know a lot about being crippled."

He flushed, his forehead creased in dismay. He moved to straighten, and groaned.

A wave of sympathy washed over her. He had to be suffering. She'd almost been a teenager when she'd fallen out of a tree and broke her leg, damaging the growth plate. Her pain had been excruciating, but she got around fine now. He looked pale with pain. No wonder his mood was dark. "Can I help—"

He lifted his hand to warn her off. "*Nee*. I'm perfectly capable of getting myself up. I've had plenty of practice."

He rose and towered over her. He had to be at least six feet tall, with broad shoulders and a slim waist.

The smell of burning eggs reached Molly's nose. She gasped as she turned and saw smoke rising from the overheated frying pan. "Your eggs! Now look what you've made me do." She pulled the pan off the burner and then turned back, ready to do verbal battle with the wretched man.

Unsteady on his feet, Isaac Graber hobbled across the kitchen floor and stepped out the back door, waving gray smoke out of his face as he shut it behind him with a slam.

Chapter Two

A gust of wind accompanied Ulla Ziegler through the back door. She hurried into the kitchen, the folds of her once-clean apron smeared with mud and brimming with a load of gritty brown potatoes and freshly pulled carrots. Fat rain drops spattered against the kitchen window.

Finishing the last of the breakfast dishes, Molly stopped mid-swipe. To her amazement her stout little mother, who slipped and slid through the door, managed to make it across the room without dropping one potato.

Molly's brow rose in agitation. Her *mamm*'s plain black shoes had left a trail of gooey brown mud across the recently mopped linoleum floor. Naturally her mother made no apologies for the added work.

Wiping her hands dry, Molly couldn't help but smirk. The sudden morning shower had turned her *mamm*'s wooly gray hair into a wild riot of curls around her untidy, limp prayer *kapp*.

A natural trader, the older woman was blessed with the gift of bartering and had bragged at breakfast about the promise of ten pounds of freshly dug potatoes from old Chicken John, a local chicken farmer, for six jars of their newly canned peaches. Molly had a feeling the old farmer had more than peaches on his mind when it came to her mother. She'd noticed the way the widower looked at her, not that Ulla gave the man much encouragement. Her *mamm* seemed satisfied with being a widow with no man to tell her what to do.

Isaac Graber came back into the house moments after Ulla, the wind catching the door and slamming it again as he fell into the closest kitchen chair. The renter jerked a handkerchief from his trouser pocket and wiped rain from his pale face.

Sniffing, Ulla took in a long, noisy breath and coughed on the kitchen's putrid air. She dumped the potatoes into a wicker basket in the corner of the big kitchen and twirled.

"What'd you burn, *dochder*?" She jerked a

dish towel off its peg and pressed it to her lips. Her watering blue-eyed gaze sliced from Molly, who stood transfixed in front of the cast iron sink, to the smoldering frying pan floating in a sea of sudsy dishwater.

Molly shrugged. She would not lie. She wanted to, but she'd never been good at weaving believable tales. Best to tell the truth. "The eggs got away from me."

She waited for her mother's reaction, her gaze slanting Isaac Graber's way, daring him to deny the truth of her words. Had he had a chance to tell her *mamm* about what had happened this morning? She looked at the bump on his forehead and then glanced away. If her *mamm* made a fuss, she surely wouldn't get to the singing practice on time.

Ulla looked in the kitchen trash and made a face, her full lips turned down at the corners. "You know it's a sin to waste good food. That dog hanging around out back would have eaten those, burned or not."

Ulla began to flap the dish towel around the room, propelling the smoke toward the slightly opened kitchen window.

"Molly didn't forget the eggs, Mrs. Ziegler." Isaac smiled and flashed his straight, white teeth. His green eyes sparkled with sincerity.

"She helped me get off the floor when I tripped over my own big feet. The eggs paid the price for her efforts. Isn't that right, Molly?"

Why was he taking up for her? She put her hands on her hips and looked him over. Pale and slender, he reclined in the old kitchen chair as calm as could be, his crutches leaning against the wall behind him. He smiled at her and her stomach flip-flopped. She went back to scrubbing the frying pan's scorched bottom. Seconds later she glanced back up at him and caught him staring at her. What was he up to?

She'd expected him to be full of tales and *gretzing* to her *mamm* about this morning, and there he sat, being nice, even generous of heart. The man kept her off-kilter, and she wasn't having any of it. "*Ya*, like he said, *Mamm*. He fell and I helped him up."

One of Ulla's gray brows spiked. She mumbled, "*Ya*, well. No matter. It's *gut* you were here to help."

Molly's gaze drifted from her *mamm*'s suspicious expression back to Isaac's calm grin. He had the nicest smile.

Ulla opened the cupboard door and asked, "You two want *kaffi*?"

"*Ya.*" Molly nodded and went back to scrubbing the pans.

Moments later mugs of steaming coffee and plates of buttered biscuits, with a dab of home-made raspberry jelly, appeared on the cluttered kitchen table. Molly sat next to her mother and looked at their new tenant. He gazed over his mug at her. A smile lit his face. She looked away, concentrating on spreading jam on her hot biscuit.

"Herr Graber tells me he bought the old bike shop yesterday and got it for a good price." Ulla shoved half of her late-morning snack in her mouth and began to chew.

"Did he?" Molly blew on her hot coffee.

"Please call me Isaac." He glanced at Molly, his green eyes bright.

Distracted by their shine, she took a gulp of coffee and burned her tongue, but would have died a million deaths before she let on. She would not give him the satisfaction of know-ing he had once again disturbed her.

"I thought since Herr Graber had some is-sues with his crutches this morning, it might be *gut* if you went with him when he takes a look at the shop." Ulla drained the last of her coffee and placed the mug on the table.

"You bought the shop sight unseen?" Molly asked.

Isaac nodded. "I did."

Foolish man. She turned to her mother and tried to keep the whine out of her voice. "I'd love to help Herr Graber, but singing practice is today. There's a frolic in a few weeks. I promised I'd come this time." Molly watched her *mamm* stuff the last crumbs of her biscuit in her mouth and sighed. She knew the *mox nix* expression her *mamm* wore. There'd be no singing practice for her today.

"I'm sure I can—" Isaac tried to interject.

Ulla rose from her chair. "It is settled. No more chatter from either of you." She dusted crumbs off her generous bust and headed for the sink, not giving Molly or Isaac another glance as she continued talking. "You are a paying guest, Herr Graber, and an Amish man in good standing with the community. Molly will be glad to help you while you stay here. She has nothing better to do."

Nothing better to do! Molly held her breath, praying she wouldn't say the angry words begging to come out of her mouth. As long as she lived in her *mamm*'s *haus*, she'd never have a say in her own comings and goings.

Molly stole a look at the dark-haired tenant and was amazed to see a hangdog expression turning his bruised forehead into a deep furrow. Maybe he didn't want her to go with him.

She pulled at her prayer *kapp*, content in knowing the idea of her tagging along was an irritation to the infuriating man. Molly put on her sweetest smile and purred, "*Ya*, I'll take him. I can always go to practice next week. We wouldn't want Herr Graber to fall again."

Isaac balanced himself on one crutch as he wedged himself between the peeling garage wall and the rusty old golf cart. He eyed the cart's front tire and gave it a tap with the toe of his boot. "How old is this contraption anyway?" Not completely convinced the rusty bucket would move with both their weight on board, he tossed his crutches in the big metal basket behind the bench seat and struggled to climb in. One hip on the cart's bench seat, he scooted over as far as he could, giving Molly plenty of room to drive.

Molly gathered up the folds of her skirt and climbed in on the driver's side. She kept her eyes looking forward, ignoring his questions about the cart. She started the engine. The machine sputtered for a moment, but then took off down the pebbled driveway with a roar.

Wind blew off his black hat. It dropped into the basket at the back of the cart. He held on and sucked in his breath as she took a corner too fast. Her prayer *kapp* fluttered against her head. The sound of glass breaking invaded his thoughts, the flashback so real it could have been happening again.

His breath quickened.

His heart pounded.

He practiced the relaxation techniques he'd been taught in the hospital, pushing away the memories of his leg twisted unnaturally under him.

Breathe deep and hold.

Traffic slowed, and he loosened his grip on the seat. Why were there no seat belts on these contraptions?

They drove through the tiny town of Pinecraft. Bahia Vista Street came up within a matter of minutes. Isaac thanked *Gott* for their safe arrival as Molly pulled into the driveway of a small strip mall and parked around the back of the little bike shop squeezed in between a fancy pizzeria and a Laundromat desperately in need of some paint. Isaac got out on his good leg, grabbed for his crutches as he wobbled like a toddler, fighting for balance.

"Here. Let me help." Molly shoved his left crutch farther under his arm, handed him his blown-off hat and walked across the minuscule patch of paved driveway toward the shop's wooden back door.

Determined to be independent, Isaac took a step. Pain shot up his leg. He stifled a moan and kept putting one foot in front of the other, leaning heavily on his crutches for support. The doctors said the pain would soon go away. The broken leg held together with nuts and bolts would finish healing. But he would always have a limp.

A split second in time had taken Thomas's life and turned the past two months into the most miserable period in his life. He'd expected more of himself, of the surgery that was supposed to put him back on his feet. He was lucky to be alive. Painful memories pushed their way in again. The sound of an ambulance screamed in his head. He pushed the sound away and took in a deep, shuttering breath.

"The door's locked. Do you have the key?" Molly asked, rattling the handle. She glanced his way, but seemed to avoid looking directly at him.

Isaac nodded. "The Realtor said it should be under this." He carefully shoved away a pail of murky motor oil with his good foot. He bent to grab the silvery key, swayed and then felt surprisingly strong arms go round his waist to steady him.

Molly stood against him, her breath tickling his ear for long seconds. She made sure he was stable and then gradually released his body. Without a word she stepped away, pulled back her skirt and grabbed for the key covered in muck.

"You do the honors. This is your new business." Molly handed him the key and then gave him room to maneuver closer to the door.

This business purchase had been on impulse, something he probably should have thought more about. He normally would have, but he'd been desperate for a reason to get up every morning. A reason to keep living.

His hand shook as he pushed open the door. He felt around for a light switch, found it, then flicked it on. A bare bulb lit the dark, cavernous bike shop with harsh light. Broken and bent bike parts, torn golf-cart seats and rusting tools lay strewed across a filthy concrete floor. Total chaos. He faltered at the door. Another fine mess he'd got himself into.

"Was isht?" Molly glanced around him and then said, "Oh!"

"Ya, oh." Isaac maneuvered around scattered bike wheels and seats, carefully picking his

way through the rubble that was Pinecraft Bike Rental and Repair. "This is what I get for buying sight unseen. What a *zot* I am."

Molly walked around him, surveying the clutter. She looked Isaac's way, her expressive brown eyes wide open.

He knew pity when he saw it. His stomach lurched. He didn't want or deserve her pity. He'd earned everything bad that happened to him. Let *Gott*'s retribution rain down on him.

"You're not a fool, Isaac. We all act impulsively sometimes. We'll get this place fixed up in no time. You'll see." She grinned, her face flushed pink.

"We?" he asked, unable to resist the urge to tease her, to take his mind off his misery.

Molly turned her back to him and moved away. "*Ya*, we. The church. Pinecraft. This community. We always pull together. You are part of us now. You'll see. *Gott* expects us to help each other." Molly went into the small office with a half wall that looked ready to fall with the least provocation.

He watched a blush creep down Molly's neck. She was young and beautiful in her own quiet way, not that he let her good looks affect him. She had no business being nice to him. She didn't know him, know who he was, what he'd done. She'd soon lose interest when she found out the truth about his past.

"I'm good with numbers," she offered. "If you need help with the books..." She turned, a ledger in hand, her gaze steady. "I'm available."

In the past Isaac would have grinned from ear to ear if a young woman had advised she was available, but he was hearing what he wanted to hear in her words. Not what she'd really meant. There was no way someone like Molly would show interest in a man like him. "*Danke*. Let's see if I get this business going before we worry about receipts and ledgers."

"I need to tell you something," Molly murmured, seeking his gaze, her look sincere.

"*Ya?*"

"*Danke* for not telling my *mamm* about how you got the bump on your head."

"*Ya*, well. I told her it happened when I fell." He picked up a box of rubber bands and set them on a small desk in the corner of the dusty room. Brooding thoughts assailed him. He pulled off his hat and pushed the painful memories away.

"You shouldn't have lied for me." Her brow arched. "There was no need. *Gott* will be—"

"Disappointed in me?" he interrupted, finishing her sentence. "Too late, Molly. He's already more disappointed than you can imagine."

"We have only to ask and *Gott* will forgive us," Molly said, holding his gaze.

He turned away, pretending to be busy with clearing the desk of trash. He wanted *Gott's* forgiveness more than he wanted air to breathe, but did he have the right to expect forgiveness after what he'd done?

"Does it hurt?"

"What?" He turned back toward her.

"The bump."

"Nee." He flipped through a pile of papers on the desk, forcing his gaze down. The bump did hurt, but he wasn't going to tell her. Some things were best left unsaid.

"The swelling is going down some."

He grinned. "I had a good nurse."

Molly laughed out loud, her eyes twinkling with mischief. "I usually try to keep my tenants as healthy as I can."

"You mean when you're not smacking them with a broom handle."

She was a tiny woman, not much taller than his little sister back in Missouri. He didn't understand why he enjoyed watching Molly bristle so much, but the frown now puckering her forehead made him grin.

"*Ya*, well. You know I didn't mean to hurt you, Isaac Graber," she muttered, jerking on her *kapp* ribbons with an air of indignation and scooted out of the little office space. When he checked on her again, she was busy wiping down shelves and stacking old parts manuals the previous owner had left behind.

Isaac chastised himself as he flopped into the office chair, the pain in his leg telling him he'd have to slow down or regret it that night. "I'm sorry for teasing you, Molly. I know you didn't mean to hurt me. My leg hurts, and the pain makes me grumpy."

She walked over to where he was sitting, a dust rag hanging from her fingertips, her brows arched. She looked at the knee he was rubbing. "How did you injure it?"

He had discussed the crash with his *daed*, *bruder*, the bishop and elders of the church, but he wasn't about to tell Molly how someone had died because of his stupidity. He turned back to the desk, lifting a big sales journal out of the desk drawer. "There's not much to tell. There was an accident. I got hurt, went to the hospital for a while and had two surgeries. The doctor said the pain will go away in time."

He forced a grin as he placed the book on the desk and pushed it her way. "Look at this. Whoever owned this place cleared out in a hurry. Wonder what the rush was?"

"Leonard Lapp owned the shop for years. I heard he retired and moved back to Ohio. His son took over the business a couple of years ago. I never met him, but rumors spread like wildfire here in Pinecraft. Some said he married an *Englischer* and abandoned the church, his faith and his *daed*'s business, too." Molly looked down at the book and then at Isaac, searching his face, her curiosity about him evident in her expression. She started to speak again, seemed to think better of it and turned away. She busied herself again. He couldn't help but watch her movements. She had a way about her, something that drew him to her like a moth to a flame.

He'd have to stay away from Molly Ziegler.

Chapter Three

Wide awake at four o'clock in the morning, Molly heard the insistent ring of another late-night caller. She sat up in bed and stretched toward the tiny cell phone approved by her bishop for midwife work. Her fingers searched the bedside table, hurrying to stop the cell phone's ring before it woke the whole house.

"*Ya*. This is Molly." She pushed back her sheet, put her feet on the cool floor and rose. "Are you timing the contractions, Ralf?" She laughed, reaching for the dress she kept hanging for nights like this. "*Ya*, I guess you're right. Six kids are plenty of practice. I'll see you in a few minutes."

She slipped on her simple work dress and work apron, then slid the phone into her medical case. She brushed back her tangled hair with fast strokes and then pinned it up in a tight bun before adding her *kapp*.

There was reason to hurry. Bretta, her friend since school, gave birth faster each time she had another child, and this birth would make number seven. There was no time for much more than a quick brush of her teeth, and she'd better be out the door.

She scurried down the hall, past Isaac's door. Did his bump still hurt. She had no cause for guilt, but she still felt at fault every time she looked at the goose egg on his forehead. Grabbing her medical bag, she pulled open the back door, ran to her cart and shoved in the key. In light drizzle she pumped the gas pedal. The golf-cart engine sputtered and coughed. *Oh, no. Not now.* She'd never make it in time if she had to run all the way to Bretta's house.

Isaac repaired engines and fixed bikes, didn't he? He would know what to do.

Molly raced through the clapboard house and down the narrow hall. She tapped lightly on Isaac's door and then began to bang harder. Time passed. Time she didn't have. "Isaac. Are you awake? Isaac?"

A sound of something falling came from the room.

"Is the house burning?" Isaac asked through the closed door.

Molly pressed her cheek to the cool wood. "No, of course it's not."

"Then go away."

Persistence was called for. She banged again. "I need your help, Isaac. Please."

The door cracked open an inch.

She couldn't see much of his face, but she could hear his heavy breathing. Had he fallen again? "I'm sorry to wake you, but there's an emergency. My cart won't start."

His door opened a bit more. She could barely make out his form in the dark hallway. "What kind of emergency? Is your *mamm* hurt?"

Molly groaned. "No. Not *Mamm*. It's Bretta. She's in labor." She heard him yawn.

"Who's Bretta?"

"There is no time for foolish chatter. I need you to help me get the cart started."

"*Outen* the lights before you try to start the engine. Your battery is probably as old as the cart."

"I tried that, Isaac. All I got was a sputter for my efforts."

She could see him run his fingers through his hair in the gloom. "And tell me why you are going out in the dark, to this woman Bretta at this hour? Is she your sister?"

"*Nee*, not my sister. My patient."

"I didn't know you were a doctor." He cleared his throat and coughed, his voice raspy.

"She's in labor. I'm her midwife. Please, Isaac. I don't have time for all these questions. I need your help now. If you're not inclined to help, just tell me. I'll call Mose."

"This Mose? Is he someone you're courting?"

Molly had no patience for all this *nix nootzing.* "Look. I'm sorry I woke you. Go back to bed." She rushed down the hall and back out the kitchen door. Where was a hero when a girl needed one? The term hero certainly didn't apply to the impressive Herr Isaac Graber. *All looks and no charm.*

Flipping on the outside light, Molly rushed over to the cart, intending to give it one last chance before running the six long blocks to Bretta's home.

She listened to the sluggish effort of the engine and groaned.

"Do you have gas in this lump of rust?" Isaac appeared out of the shadows and leaned on the cart, one crutch under his arm. He breathed hard and fast.

"Gas?" Had she remembered to fill the tank after their outing to the bike shop? *Nee.* She turned the key, looked at the tank's gauge. Empty. What a *bensel* she was. No gas and a *mamm*-to-be waiting. Worse still, Isaac grinned like he knew what a *bensel* she was. "I forgot to fill the tank. What am I going to do? I have no choice but to run all the way, or disturb Mose."

"Stop panicking and listen. Does your *mamm* keep gas around for the lawn mower?"

"I don't know. Our neighbor, Herr Zucker, cuts the grass, but he does use our mower." Molly headed for the shed just inside the fenced backyard. She pulled a long string on the wall. Light pooled a golden glow around her. She lifted a gas can off the metal shelf, shook it and then ran back to the cart.

Isaac stood barefoot next to the cart, his pajama bottoms soaking up the dampness from the grass underfoot. He had the cart's gas cap in his hand.

She avoided looking directly at him and poured the gas in the cart's tank. Isaac screwed on the cap and then surveyed her from head to toe. "You don't look like any midwife I've ever seen."

"And how many have you seen?" Molly asked, sliding into the driver's seat.

He scratched his head and yawned wide. "Only you."

She started the sluggish engine and began to slowly back up. "Thank you so much, Isaac."

"I didn't do anything. Just took off the gas cap and put it back on." He started walking toward the back door, his one crutch taking all his weight.

"You saved the day and you know it," she called over her shoulder and drove off into the night, her medical bag bouncing in the basket.

Glancing back, she watched the glow from the house light turn Isaac into a dark shadow as he slipped into the back door, his shoulders stooped. Why did the man have such a hard time accepting compliments? Didn't he realize how important it was to have a midwife arrive before the baby? She smiled as she drove on into the darkness. Whether he wanted to admit it to himself or not, he was her hero tonight, and she'd show him her appreciation somehow.

"Food's up."

Molly scrubbed the last of the dried egg yolk off the table and headed toward the kitchen's service window. Each step was painful. The new shoes she'd bought on sale tested her patience. She couldn't wait to get home, take them off and soak her feet in a hot tub of shiny, fragrant bubbles.

Willa Mae, the owner of the popular cafe since Hurricane Katrina had displaced her, stuck a sprig of parsley on the edge of the plate of steaming home fries and perfect over-easy eggs. She pushed it toward Molly. "Table six, and make it snappy. He seems in a hurry."

Putting on her friendly waitress smile, Molly took the plate and hurried over to the lone man sitting in the front booth by the door. His back to her, she placed the large plate in front of the newspaper the dark-haired man was reading and cheerfully rattled off, "Here you go. Fries and eggs. Hope you enjoy them."

"I would have enjoyed them more ten minutes ago." The man's hand rattled his empty coffee mug to express his neglect.

"I'm so sorry, sir. We've been a bit busy and I…Isaac? *Was tut Sie Hier?*"

Pulling his plate closer, he folded his newspaper and looked at Molly. "Why do you think I'm here? I'm hungry and want my second cup of coffee."

She hadn't seen Isaac since he'd repaired the cart for her the day before. "Why didn't you eat at home? *Mamm* made pancakes with hot apple-butter early this morning."

"I'm a solitary man. I like my own company," he grumbled as he cut his eggs into perfect bite-sized squares. He leaned over the plate to get the full benefit of a fork full of eggs and home fries. "Now, can I have some coffee to wash down my breakfast?"

"*Ya*, of course. I'll get you coffee right away."

Taking a fresh carafe of coffee off the heater, Molly hurried back, reminding herself of the café's customer service policy. *The customer is always right.* She'd agreed with the policy when she'd taken the job a year ago, but some days it took perseverance and a cool head to be friendly and courteous to certain patrons who passed through the café door.

She grimaced as the toe of her built-up shoe hit the edge of Isaac's booth, but kept a smile plastered on her face. "Let me pour you a fresh cup of coffee." She went to pour, and before she could stop him, he reached for the tiny container of milk next to his cup.

Hot coffee splashed his wrist and shirt cuff. He jerked his hand away and reached for a napkin. "Do you really work here, or are you following me around, making sure I get hurt at least once a day?"

She spoke before she thought, her temper spiked by her throbbing toes and his grumpy words. "Has anyone ever pointed out how rude you are?" She put the carafe on the table harder than necessary. Her hands on her narrow hips, she glared at him, her smile gone. "If not, let me be the first. You are no ray of sunshine, Isaac Graber, and in future I'll make sure another waitress comes to your table to abuse you."

"That's fine." He sipped at his coffee and completely ignored her.

"Fine." Molly turned on her heel and marched back to her section of the café, her fists clenched, and feeling more like a petulant child than a grown woman.

Willa Mae flipped several pancakes and then motioned Molly over to the service window. "You're as red as summer sandals. What happened? That guy get fresh with you?"

"That guy is Isaac Graber, one of my *mamm*'s new boarders. Sometimes he makes me so mad."

"Let me guess. Did he pinch your backside, child?"

"No, not at all. He's…" Molly's voice trailed off as she searched for the right word. "He's not exactly weird, you know, just kind of friendly one minute and helpful and then he goes all strange and acts the fool."

"Oh. I get it. He's not showing enough interest in you and you're mad."

Molly straightened her *kapp*, tied her apron on a bit tighter and snapped, "*Nee*, that's not it at all. He keeps accusing me of hurting him on purpose, like I spend my whole day thinking up ways to cause him pain."

"You hitting on my customers?"

"You know perfectly well I'm not. Well… I did hit him in the head with a dust mop the other day, but that was completely his fault, not mine."

Sliding a plate of golden pancakes Molly's way, Willa Mae smiled, her dark weave shiny after standing over the hot grill all morning. "This story just keeps getting better and better. Tell me everything. When are you two making your announcement in church?"

Molly shot her best friend and boss a look that said it all. "These pancakes go to your gentleman at table six. Enjoy!" Willa Mae grinned.

Four hours later a midday band of rain swept in from the coast, surprising Isaac and leaving him a prisoner in his own shop. An hour passed. Not one customer came through the shop door. His early-morning meal at the café was nothing but a pleasant memory.

He rubbed his stomach. The wonderful aroma of hot pizza mingled with the less appealing odors of grease and dirt, but still his stomach stirred. An hour later it continued to rumble loudly, begging for lunch. He downed another bottle of water and tried not to think about food, especially the pizza shop next door. He wasn't about to trust his leg and poor balance on the slippery sidewalk outside. He would wait until the rain stopped.

There wasn't much he could do to pass the time while still on crutches. He called several cleaning businesses and wrote down price quotes. Sticker shock took away some of his appetite. The amounts asked to clear out the trash from the old building was enough to buy another electric golf cart. He'd need more carts to lease to the snowbirds pouring into Pinecraft from the north. The winter tourist season would quickly pass. Every day the bike shop wasn't open he was losing money—money he needed for a permanent place to live.

A feeling of defeat swamped him as he looked around the shop, at shelves falling off the walls, trash littering the floor. An ache began to thump at the base of his skull.

The roar of a high octane engine pulling up to the curb outside drew his attention. He rose, shoving aside pieces of a dismantled blue cart in order to maneuver toward the front door. He leaned against one crutch as he wiped away some of the dried white paint swirled on the storefront windows to block out the sun.

The side door of a black van labeled Fischer Transport opened and he was surprised to see Molly jumping to the pavement, followed by several stocky Amish men. Women in tidy prayer *kapps* and plain dresses in a variety of shapes and colors followed close behind. Isaac opened the shop door and was inundated with slaps on the back, smiling faces and so many introductions he'd never remember them all.

Busy shaking hands with the men and nodding to the women, Isaac took time to glance at Molly and return her enthusiastic grin. Her warm brown eyes seemed to be saying, *you didn't think I'd leave you to clean up this mess on your own, did you?*

A tall, curly-haired blond man with powerful shoulders and a firm handshake squeezed Isaac's hand. "*Willkumm* to Pinecraft, Herr Graber. I'm Mose Fischer and this is my *bruder*'s son, Wilhelm. I've heard a lot about you from Molly. I thought I'd come see this *youngie* she speaks of so fondly, with his fine mind for motors and winning personality."

Isaac nodded at the tall man and the skinny teenage boy standing next to him and smiled his welcome as he readjusted the crutch shaken loose from under his arm. "Molly's been talking to you about me?"

"*Ya*, she has. Nasty bump you've got there."

Isaac's gaze skimmed the bland expression Molly directed his way. Had she told him what really happened? As if feeling guilty, she looked down, busying herself with a pile of magazines on the floor. "*Ya*. Like a *bensel* I fell over my own feet."

"So I heard." Mose winked, telling Isaac he knew what had really happened. "I hope you don't mind us coming to help. We may live in a tourist town, but I think you'll find Pinecraft's a strong Amish community, ready to help out in times of need." He slapped Isaac on the back. "Besides, I have an ulterior motive. One of my little girls has a bike that needs a tube replaced, and I don't have time to work on it. You'll find we do a lot of bike riding around here. There's a real need for this shop to be up and running, for the community's sake, as well as your own."

Isaac looked around at the smiling people. They all seemed ready to work. He sent a grin of appreciation Molly's way. She'd gathered this mob of workers for him, even though he'd been rude to her at breakfast this morning. He owed her a debt of gratitude. He'd find a way to pay her kindness.

Mose pulled on the arm of an *Englischer* man in jeans and a white T-shirt who was busy working on organizing parts against the wall. "Let me introduce you to one of our local police officers, Bradley Ridgeway."

Smiling, his arm full of bike tubes and tires, Officer Ridgeway extended his free hand. "Glad to meet you, Isaac. Anytime you need help, you just let me know. I've got two sons who love their bikes. They're going to be glad to hear the bike shop's opening again."

Isaac shook the man's hand, but shame made him avoid looking directly in his eyes. *"Danke,"* Isaac managed to croak out. He turned away, pretending to be looking for something in the old desk in the office.

Molly moved close to him. He watched her as she and a well-rounded, middle-aged woman navigated a cluster of men working along the back wall. She caught his eye and motioned for him to join them.

"This is Becky Esch, our local baker," Molly said, and linked her arm through the woman's.

The older Amish woman smiled up at him, her startling blue eyes reminding him of his mother. Heavyhearted, Isaac nodded, quickly pushing away the momentary sadness that threatened to overwhelm him. "Ah...you must have been the one who made those wonderful doughnuts someone was passing around," he said.

"*Ya*, well. Single men need nourishment, I always say, especially when they're working this hard. I have an idea. Why don't you come eat dinner with us some Saturday night? The girls and I could use some company. We get lonesome now that Zelner's passed on to be with the Lord. It'll be nice to have a man at the head of our table for a change."

He glanced at Molly. The people crowded into the bike shop were her friends, not his. He wasn't sure what to say, but relaxed when Molly grinned at him with a twinkle in her eyes. "*Ya*, sure," he said. "That would be fine. *Danke*."

"*Gut*. The girls and I will expect you at six next Saturday. And make sure you bring your appetite."

As the woman walked away, Molly giggled under her breath and poked him in the rib.

"What's so funny?" he whispered, his head tilting her way.

"You have no idea what you just stepped into," Molly said, laughing with all the joy of a five-year-old. "Becky Esch has two old-maid daughters and she's just set a trap for you."

"You could have warned me," Isaac scolded.

Molly's brows went up as her smile deepened. "I could have," she said, then straightened the ribbons on her *kapp* as she turned her back on him and shouldered her way through the throng of workers.

Isaac's eyes narrowed as he noticed the slight limp in her gait. He didn't know what to think of their push-pull relationship, but knew he'd better work harder at keeping his distance from her. Molly was the kind of woman he'd choose if he were looking for someone to court. But after what he'd done to Thomas, there was no chance he would risk getting married any time soon. If ever.

Chapter Four

Molly hummed as she worked for an hour in the hot kitchen, preparing rosemary pork chops, roasted new potatoes with chives and fresh green beans slathered in butter and onion sauce for later that night. A homemade cheesecake drizzled in thick strawberry syrup sat waiting on the kitchen counter. The meal begged for her *mamm* to come home with an appetite, but at 6:00 p.m. the house remained quiet and still.

Dinnertime came and went. Darkness shrouded the plain, wood-framed house, the only home she had ever known. The old clock in the front room chimed seven times before Molly rose from the kitchen table, flipped on the light over the sink and stored the uneaten meal into containers. She cleaned up the dirty pans and was wiping the last of the crumbs off the counter as Isaac walked through the back door, his face etched with tired lines from his long day at work.

"Something sure smells *gut* in here. Am I too late for dinner?"

Molly beamed, her mood lifting, glad for company and conversation, even if it was only Isaac. "*Nee*, not at all." She pulled out a kitchen chair. "Come. Sit. Let me heat some food for you."

Isaac removed his hat and tossed it on the spare kitchen chair. He ran his fingers though his hair before he sat. "No other houseguests tonight?"

"*Nee*. Our last short-term guest left early this morning. She's on her way to see her sister in Lakeland, but she'll probably stop for another night with us on her way back to Ohio. Seems everyone else went to Pinecraft Park for the bluegrass singing tonight." She pulled the containers of food out of the refrigerator and then turned back to Isaac, her curiosity getting the better of her. "Is the shop ready to be opened yet?"

"I think so. I still need some parts, but they should get here in a few days."

He flashed a grin at her that played havoc with Molly's insides. She ignored the feeling and shoved their plates into the still-hot oven. "*Gott* brought you here. He'll make sure the customers come through the doors, Isaac. We have to trust His will. Why don't you clean up a bit while the food's heating?"

He looked down at his dusty clothes and reached for his crutches. "*Gut* idea. I think I will." He rose, wincing as he put his weight on his leg. "I won't be long."

She watched him lumber out of the kitchen, his limp more noticeable than it had been in days. Her heart went out to him. Pain was a lousy friend. She knew. She'd lived with it long enough.

Turning on another light to dispel the nuance of an intimate setting, she puttered around the kitchen, putting an extra place mat on the table, then some silverware. A tub of locally made butter was set in the middle of the table.

She stood still for a moment, listening to the sounds Isaac made at the back of the house. Just as she put down the bread plates and poured tall glasses of cold milk, he hurried back into the kitchen wearing clean work clothes, his hair slicked back from his thin face.

"I hope you don't mind if we eat in the kitchen. It's just you and me tonight," Molly said. "I waited for *Mamm*, but she must have gotten held up." Her mother usually served the last meal of the day in the more formal dining room, around the big wooden table that was large enough to seat twelve for Thanksgiving and Christmas.

Isaac returned to the chair he'd been sitting in moments before and leaned his crutches close by. "*Ya*, sure. Here is fine," he said, taking a sip of milk.

She pulled the rack of reheated chops out of the stove. "I hope you like stuffed pork chops."

"I do. They're my favorite," he murmured, watching her.

She placed the largest chop on Isaac's warmed plate. "Would you like some cinnamon?" A bottle of the tangy spice hovered over the generous mound of homemade applesauce Molly had served him.

He nodded. "Sounds *gut*." He tucked his napkin on his lap.

Molly carried the two plates she'd prepared to the table and placed one in front of Isaac before sitting across from him. "Salt and pepper is on the table if you need it."

He glanced at the salt shaker close to him and then glanced back at her, a slight smile turning up the corners of his mouth. "Before we pray I want to thank you for all the help you brought to the shop today."

"I'm glad we could contribute," Molly said, not wanting to delve into her own motives too deeply. She owed him. That was all. He wasn't the only one who could be a hero.

"You did more than help. I would have never been able to get the shop as clean and organized as it is now without all those additional hands. I owe you, and the kind people of Pinecraft."

"All I did was call my brother-in-law, Mose. Once he heard about your situation, he made the calls and did the rest."

"So Mose is family?" Isaac asked.

"*Ya*, he was married to my sister, Greta, but she went home to be with the Lord three years ago."

"I'm sorry for your loss."

She was surprised by the sound of sincerity in Isaac's voice. Memories of Greta, her smile, the way she found good in everyone, came rushing back. Molly took a deep breath and ignored the pain prodding her heart. With a jerk of her head, she nodded. "Thank you, Isaac. I still miss her, but *Gott* had a plan. We don't always understand, but we will once we can sit down and talk with Him."

"Let's pray so we can eat," Isaac suggested, and bowed his head.

Moments later Molly lifted her chin and found herself grinning as Isaac tore into his food with the gusto of a starving man.

"That strawberry cheesecake on the counter looks special. Somebody's birthday today?" he asked, his eyes shifting back to Molly. He sliced off a large piece of pork chop and stuck it into his mouth.

"*Ya*. Mine."

"Happy birthday! How old are you?"

She dipped her head, ashamed to admit she was so old and still not married. "Twenty-one, but it's no big deal. *Mamm* and I usually just celebrate alone with a home-cooked meal when it's one of our birthdays." Molly clasped her hands in her lap, putting on a bright smile she didn't feel.

"Birthdays are always special, Molly. Especially when it's your twenty-first."

"*Ya*, I guess," she murmured, her appetite disappearing. "It's such a big deal, *Mamm* didn't bother to show up for the event," she muttered.

"I'm sorry."

Molly tucked into her potatoes, determined

to change the subject. "*Ya*, well, it doesn't matter." *Not to* Mamm *it doesn't.*

A half hour later Ulla placed her purse on the cleared kitchen table, along with a small bag from the new bookstore in town. "I've been with John all day," she said casually. "How was your day, Molly?"

"Fine." Molly stayed quiet. Isaac had gone to bed, and she'd been left to finish the last of the cleaning up.

"Have you heard from Samuel today? He wanted to know when you two could start courting."

"I have no interest in Samuel, *Mamm*. I told you this already."

"Well, he has an interest in you, and I think it's time you begin to show an interest in him."

Molly ignored her *mamm* and left the kitchen, her head held high. It was her birthday, and all her mother could do was talk of Samuel Bawell. She had forgotten her birthday completely. Not that her forgetting was anything new or surprising. She often forgot Molly existed, unless there was a chore to be done that she didn't want to do herself. Molly was still treated like an unwanted child, and she was tired of it.

Greta had always been her mother's favorite daughter. When Greta died in childbirth, Beatrice and Mercy, Mose and Greta's tiny daughters, had taken her sister's place of importance in her mother's heart. Molly didn't blame the girls. They were beautiful, like their mother, not plain like her. The *bobbels* were blessings from *Gott*. She adored them like any devoted aunt would. They were innocent children and had no idea their *grossmammi* played favorites and made her younger daughter feel inferior.

Molly closed her bedroom door and leaned against it. Tears began to flow until her eyes burned with grit. She hated when people wallowed in self-pity, and here she was feeling sorry for herself, with a great big hole in her heart.

In the dark she walked across the small room and sat at her dressing table. With the flick of her wrist, she turned on her lamp and pulled the pins from her *kapp* and bun. She massaged her scalp, her blond hair falling like a heavy curtain down her back. Reluctantly she looked into the mirror. Her eyes were puffy, her lashes dark with tears. Her nose was red in the semidarkness of the room. She pulled her *grossmammi*'s brush through the tangles on her head and winced as it caught in her hair. She ignored the pain and lifted her hands to braid the long strands into a thick plait.

She stared at herself in the mirror. No longer a girl, but a woman of twenty-one now. An adult...limited by one leg shorter than the other, unmarried, not being courted by a man she could love, still living with her *mamm*. Failure looked back at her in the brown eyes of the woman she'd become.

She turned off her lamp, knocking over her dressing-table stool as she rose and blindly moved toward the tallboy dresser against the wall. In the dark she grabbed a nightgown from the drawer. The soft cotton gown smelled of lilacs, homemade washing soap and good, fresh air.

Tomorrow things were going to change. She'd come up with a new plan for her life. She'd learn to stand up for herself. She had to, or she'd fast find herself married to Samuel Bawell.

The next day the bell over the door rang, announcing another customer. Isaac was filled with excitement. He'd been busy selling, renting and repairing bikes all day. He'd sold his last two secondhand golf carts and left a voice mail with his supplier, telling him he needed to purchase two more used carts for repair and sale. After today he'd have no problem paying next month's bills and still have money left over to buy a few supplies.

He looked up and was surprised to find Molly wandering around the shop. Today her pale pink dress put a healthy glow to her cheeks. She looked pretty, but then she always looked fresh and tidy to him. Even last night, with her joy robbed by her mother's failure to celebrate her birthday, she'd seemed content with his company. He wasn't sure what it was about her, but he enjoyed the way she made him feel when she was around.

He usually wasn't one to be impressed with good looks. Before he'd come to Pinecraft, a good personality always got his attention first. But Molly seemed to radiate a special light from her dark eyes. And there was something about her tiny frame that made her look frail and helpless even though she was strong and capable, with a personality to match. "I'm surprised to see you here. Shopping for a new cart? The one you drive should be put in the town dump as a relic." He smiled, waiting for reaction.

Her forehead wrinkled in response to his words. "There's nothing wrong with my cart, and this is no time for teasing, Isaac Graber. I've come to talk to you about a serious matter."

He noticed her dark eyes were red-rimmed and puffy. Concern washed over him. Over the past few days, he'd seen Molly in many moods, but nothing like this melancholy state of mind. "What's wrong?" he asked, motioning for her to sit on the old couch.

She moved a few magazines and sat. "I don't know where to start. You're probably not the right person to talk to. I don't even know if you consider me a friend." Molly's expression was grim, her mouth an angry line.

Isaac lowered himself into the seat next to her. He took her hand in his, considered the fine, delicate bones that held such strength. "*Ya*, of course you're my friend. Don't be silly. This shop wouldn't be open today if it wasn't for your thoughtfulness. You talk. I'll listen."

Molly sniffed, dabbing at her nose with her handkerchief. "My *mamm* and I had a fuss this morning." Molly took in a deep breath. "She's made a ridiculous demand, and I'm not putting up with it anymore. I've made a decision, and it might be the worst mistake I'll ever make."

Isaac thought back to the mistakes he'd made the day Thomas died. Choices that cost Thomas his life. Isaac understood regret only too well.

Hoping to cheer her up, Isaac smiled as he spoke in a teasing manner, "*Ya*, go on. Tell me about this terrible mistake you're about to make."

"It's not that easy to talk about." She looked up, and her frown deepened. "I don't know why I came here." She twisted her hand away from him. "I should go back home, take a nap. Anything to stop worrying." She tried to stand, but he pulled her back to the couch. With trembling fingers, she pushed away the wisps of hair in her face as she looked at him. "I can be such a fool, Isaac."

"You're many things, Molly Ziegler, but foolish is not one of them. I see a strong woman before me. Someone who loves deeply and has a heart of compassion. I see no fool." Their gaze held, eyes searching. Molly's brokenhearted expression tugged at his soul. He felt emotions that were foreign to him, feelings that scared and excited him. At that moment he would give her the moon if he could, anything to bring back her joy.

Molly blinked, her head turning away. "I…" She began again. "I really need your help. I know I'm asking a lot, and you can always say no, but I don't know who else to turn to, and if I don't find an answer, I could end up married to a man I don't love, maybe even be unchurched if I refuse to wed."

"Tell me what you need me to do."

Her chin dropped against her chest. "My *mamm* has plans, plans that don't set well with me."

"What sort of plans?" Isaac's stomach knotted.

"She insists I court—*nee*—marry Samuel Bawell." She tugged at her prayer *kapp* ribbon as she turned to look at him, tears pooling in her eyes. "I know everyone thinks he's such a good man, but he's not. I've seen a different side to him, one that concerns me." A single tear clung to her damp lashes and then dropped to her cheek. "He can be rough and demanding when he doesn't get his way and then go all sweet and gentle like it never happened. *Mamm* says it's just my imagination, but it's not. I won't marry him, Isaac. Not without love." Her gaze smoldered with raw, mixed emotions.

Isaac squeezed her warm hand, wishing he had the right words to comfort her. Arranged marriages still happened in his community back home, but most *youngies* picked their own mates nowadays. "She threatened to force you into this loveless marriage knowing how you feel?"

"*Ya*, and she will if it suits her purpose." She sighed deeply and slowly as she tugged at her *kapp* ribbon again, her expression grim.

"What are you going to do?" Isaac had no advice to offer Molly. He couldn't manage his own life issues. How could he help her?

"That's where you come in." She made an effort to grin at him through her tears, her cheeks flaming red. Her hand fidgeted with the handkerchief in her lap.

"Tell me," Isaac encouraged.

"If my *daed* were alive, he'd put a stop to all this nonsense…but he's not. *Mamm* has all the power. I'm just the old maid." She pushed her shoulders back and held his gaze as she sniffed. "I know it's a lot to ask of anyone, especially you, but I couldn't think of anyone else who could help." Her bottom lip began to quiver.

"I can't help if you don't tell me what you need of me," Isaac encouraged, patting her hand.

Molly took in a deep, ragged breath. "Would you pretend to court me for a little while, act like you have a real interest in me? Between the two of us, we can consider it a joke. It would mean nothing serious or binding."

Isaac's eyebrows went up in surprise.

"I know we barely know each other, and that we don't share affection in that way, but we'd only have to go places together. Be seen in public once in a while. Nothing more. Just pretend an interest to fool my mother and the community until Samuel goes back home to Ohio in a few weeks. Once he returns home, we can end the relationship. You can just tell people I wasn't the one for you."

Isaac looked at Molly, saw expectation in her eyes. Coming to him, asking him for help, couldn't have been easy for her. He couldn't let her down, not after all the help she'd given him. He owed her that much, but was still surprised when he heard himself say, "*Ya*, sure. I can do that for you. You'll let me know when you want to start this pretending?"

Molly's stressed expression relaxed. She smiled. "There's a singing frolic in the Mennonite church tonight. All the *youngies* are going. If you're not too busy…maybe we could go together and hold hands when we get there so others would see." Molly's expression grew pensive again, her smile disappearing.

"*Ya*, that sounds okay," he said, not sure he was doing the right thing.

"Thanks so much, Isaac." Molly threw her

arms around his neck, squeezed hard and then jumped off the couch. "I've got to get home before *Mamm* does. We've got a new guest, and she complains when lunch meals aren't on the table at noon."

Standing, Isaac watched Molly hurry out the shop door, a relieved smile brightening her face. He ambled back toward his chair. What had he gotten himself into?

Silence greeted him as he turned back into his office. Pain coursed down his leg, reminding him he needed to take one of the pain pills the *Englischer* doctor had given him that morning. A few days of pain medication and maybe he'd stop snapping customer's heads off just because he hurt in body as well as spirit.

He wanted to help Molly, but he didn't want to give her the wrong idea, either. She'd been nothing but good to him, but she deserved someone better to court, even if their relationship would be nothing but pretense.

Leaning forward and looking around the clean, organized bike shop took the frown off his face. He'd never experienced such kindness from total strangers before. The people of Pinecraft had been generous to a fault. Getting to know them, he found Mennonites, Amish and *Englischers* all working side by side, without pay, but with a common goal. To get his business open.

He was almost ready to flip the Closed sign over to Open, and he had Molly and the people of Pinecraft to thank for that. She'd even brought in Mose Fischer, his first real customer. And now he was about to start a fake courtship with her.

Isaac dumped his new pain pills into his hand. He looked down at the white capsules. There had been a time in his life when he'd have been tempted to swallow the whole bottle just to keep the thoughts of what he'd done to Thomas at bay, but today he singled out a pill, stuck it in his mouth and swallowed it down with a drink from his bottle of water.

Life was for the living, not that he deserved to live, but he had a reason to go on. He set the medicine bottle on his desk and picked up the phone. Maybe a reminder to his supply house would get the carts here a few days early. He'd be glad when the shop was officially open and he had something more to do with his time than sleep and eat.

The bell above the door clattered. Glancing over his shoulder, Isaac watched a man come into the shop, his shirt logo telling him the shop's new sign was finally ready to go up.

Excitement built in his heart. The bike shop would officially be open in a few days, and he was going to the singing frolic with one of the sweetest girls in Pinecraft. He had no right to the joy that overwhelmed him, but he humbly accepted it as a gift from *Gott*.

He looked down and saw Molly's handkerchief on the shop floor. He stopped and picked it up. The scent of lavender floated up and tickled his nose. Smiling, he tucked the cloth in his pocket next to his heart and hurried toward the shop door to greet a customer. Tonight when he saw Molly he'd give the square of white linen back to her. He beamed at the thought of being with her, holding her hand, but busied himself as he reminded himself their courting was for Ulla's benefit, not his.

Chapter Five

Two hours later Molly stood silently at the thrift store's front window, pretending to flip through men's shirts hanging from a metal rack, when she was really watching Isaac's bike-shop door. She couldn't stop thinking about him, about the fake courtship she'd proposed to him.

Now that she'd had time to consider the situation, she realized Isaac must think her a complete *bensel* for asking him to go along with her foolish ruse.

Why had he agreed to fake an interest in her? They hardly knew each other. Were strangers really. What was in it for him? They had nothing in common, with the exception of living in Pinecraft and both being Amish. No one was going to believe they'd fallen in love so quickly.

Her shoulders slumped. Most of the time they weren't even nice to each other.

She straightened two shirts on their plastic hangers and pondered her fate. Her mother knew her better than anyone, knew she seldom acted impulsively. Everyone in the little tourist town thought of her as good ole practical Molly, the spinster with no personal life. She was the one everyone counted on. Her forehead crinkled with irritation as she shoved a shirt across the rack with such force the plastic hanger broke and fell to the floor. She bent to retrieve it, her mind racing. Her *mamm* wasn't going to fall for their pretense unless her and Isaac's romance was very convincing. That meant she'd need Isaac's total cooperation. He was a busy shopkeeper. He didn't have time for her childish ideas. He probably thought her a silly old maid, coming up with such grand schemes just so she didn't have to marry.

Movement across the street caught her eye. She watched with interest as a big crane carried a sign toward the roof of Isaac's bike shop. The store had been called Lapp's Bike Shop for more years than she could remember. Now it would have a new name, a new beginning.

Every bike she'd ever owned had been purchased, fixed, painted or exchanged there.

She could see Isaac silhouetted in the doorway, his stiff black hat in hand, the warm tropic breezes blowing his dark hair into his eyes.

In a few days everyone in Pinecraft was supposed to believe this dark-haired, brooding man wanted to be her husband. She was growing more and more uncomfortable with the deception in which she'd tangled Isaac. But if she tried to fight her *mamm* alone, she'd lose and be forced to marry Samuel. She sighed and leaned closer to the store window, watching the sign go up into the air.

"I thought we came to look for tablecloths. Are we going to shop, or are you going to stand there all day gawking out the window?" Ruth, tall, thin and very pregnant, called from the housewares aisle a few feet away. They'd been friends all their lives and now were next-door neighbors every November through March since Ruth had married and was living in Ohio with her husband most of the year. "I've only got a couple of hours to shop. You know when Saul starts banging on the table, dinner better be ready. You coming?"

With a smile Molly held up one finger and signaled for her friend to wait. She held her breath as the crane turned the sign around. In bold black letters, on a plain white background she read the words, THE BIKE PIT. The name described the hole-in-the-wall shop to perfection. She smiled as she scurried away, pleased for Isaac and his new adventure.

"Why are you smiling? Some *Englischer* wave at you?" Ruth picked up a lovely hand-painted cup and saucer with dainty pink roses. She set the pricy old dust catcher back on the shelf.

Molly forced the smile off her face. "No, nothing like that. Just a new sign going up across the street." Molly glanced over her shoulder and peeked at the sign again.

Ruth picked up the cup and saucer again, seemed to do a considerable amount of thinking before putting it in the shopping basket hanging from her wrist. She tucked a pair of secondhand socks around the fragile memento for safekeeping. "You think I'll break this?"

"*Ya.* Probably the first time you wash it," Molly answered truthfully.

"I don't care. I'm getting it anyway, but don't tell your *mamm.* She'll spread it around that I've gone fancy."

"Well, you have, haven't you?" Molly laughed as Ruth stuck out her tongue at her and headed toward more household items, muttering, "Yeah, but that doesn't mean everyone and their sister has to know."

Molly called after her, "I think I'll pen an article to the Pinecraft Weekly. I can see the headlines now. 'Ruth Lapp Drinks Coffee Out of Bone China and Gets in Trouble for It.'"

Ruth gave Molly a scathing look, her bottom lip half curled in a smile. "You do, and I'll write one about that mysterious bump on your new tenant's head."

Molly hurried to catch up with her friend. "I told you that was purely accidental."

"That's not what Isaac Graber said while we were cleaning his shop."

"He didn't say anything about it, and you know it," Molly fired back. She pulled out a white tablecloth, saw a red wine stain and refolded the cloth, stain side up.

Feeling eyes on her, Molly glanced up and saw Isaac enter the store. He gave her a quick nod and then shifted his gaze away as he continued to walk toward the front of the store. He leaned heavily on a cane, heading for the secondhand bike rack they'd just passed. He had a hitch in his step, but otherwise appeared as fit as he had that morning. "Oh, no. Not him," Molly said.

Ruth paused, rummaging through the tablecloths long enough to admonish, "That's not nice, Margaret Anne Ziegler."

She wouldn't have to pretend with Ruth. She'd tell her friend about her and Isaac's pretend courtship when the time was right. But not today. "You don't have to live in the same house with him or share a meal when he's grumpy." Molly tossed a used but spotless tablecloth on their stack of possibilities.

"I think we ought to be nice and see if he needs help. It can't be easy shopping with one hand," Ruth murmured.

Too embarrassed to speak to him now that she'd realized he probably regretted his promise to her, Molly whispered, "You help him then. I'm staying right here."

"That's what's wrong with the world. No one's willing to help their neighbor anymore." Ruth lumbered off, her hands resting on the top of her bullet-shaped belly.

"Oh, all right. Wait up. But don't blame me if he doesn't want our help. He's funny like that."

Ruth kept walking but glanced back. "You mean he's independent?"

Molly screwed up her face and said, "Something like that."

Isaac perused the array of secondhand bikes lined up in a neat row, mentally calculating how many he could buy and still have enough money left over for meals and bike parts. He'd already bought several golf carts to use as rentals. Like most Amish, he didn't believe in credit cards or payment plans. It was cash-and-carry or do without. His savings were almost gone, but the shelves were better stocked. Several more rental bikes would keep the shop going, especially if the bike repairs kept trickling in.

The sound of laughter grabbed his attention. Molly came back into view. His stomach flip-flopped as he remembered their conversation that morning. Would anyone believe someone like Molly would choose a man like him for a husband?

He turned and glanced Molly's way. She was laughing with a woman he'd met, but he couldn't put a name to. "Let me guess," he said, hobbling up. "You've come to kick my cane out from under me."

Molly's face flushed red, as if he'd gone too far with his latest comment. "I don't know why you go about saying I hurt you on purpose."

"I was only joking, Molly. If you weren't so easily riled, I probably wouldn't have so much fun making you angry."

"Let me poke a hole in your theory, Isaac Graber. I couldn't care less what you say or do," she snapped back, their earlier camaraderie forgotten.

Ruth edged her way between the two of them. "We thought we'd come help you shop since you're one-handed today."

"That's very kind of you...I'm sorry. I'm lousy at remembering names. Refresh my memory?"

"I'm Ruth. Ruth Lapp, Saul's wife." The pregnant woman blushed a pretty pink. "Molly was just saying what a wonderful tenant you are."

Isaac snickered. "I imagine she was." He turned Molly's way, lost his balance and grabbed for a bike handle to steady himself.

His hip bumped the bike, and, like a row of dominoes, they began to fall, one by one, with horrific clangs of metal against metal.

Seconds later Isaac found himself on the cool concrete floor, in the middle of the jumble, his injured leg spared the brunt of the fall, but his masculine pride seriously damaged.

"I was nowhere near you. You can't blame this on me, Isaac," Molly said, her lips quivering, her laughter barely held in check. "Not this time..." Her voice trailed off as the store manager came and stood next to them, his arms folded across his broad chest.

Isaac's gaze veered away from Molly to the man frowning at him. "I'll take all six. Do you deliver?"

Molly pushed a red bike across the street, dodging several speeding cars, then trotting to the shop door Ruth held open for her. "You got me in more trouble."

"Did not," Ruth jeered. "You didn't have to offer to help Isaac, but you're kindhearted and a little in love with the man. It was you who said we'd help. Not me." She patted her baby bump. "The baby's really active today. I think he's going to like bikes."

"Did you see his face?

"Whose?" Ruth asked, looking confused.

"Isaac's. He looked grief-stricken, like the last thing he wanted to do was buy a pile of dented bikes."

"I thought you said he's always grumpy." Ruth lined up the bike Molly handed off to her.

"He is…well, not exactly grumpy. He's funny sometimes, and helpful…but he has this way about him. Sort of like he's miserable or unhappy."

"You want to fix him, that's your problem. We women love to fix our men." Ruth plopped down on an old, cracked leather couch positioned against the half wall of the office and sighed as if she'd been running a marathon.

Molly joined Ruth on the couch and picked at a piece of torn leather as she spoke. "That's not true. I don't want to fix him. I think he wants to fix me." Her words were out of her mouth before she could stop them.

Interested, Ruth asked, "Fix *you*? What do you mean?" She rubbed a spot on her stomach, her gaze focused on Molly's face.

Molly took off her built-up shoe and flexed her toes, avoiding Ruth's scrutiny. "*Ya*, well. I asked a favor of him and he agreed to help because he knows I'm a fool, that's all."

"Help? In what way?"

"With a courting ruse." Molly worried the ribbon of her *kapp*. She wished she'd kept her mouth shut. She intended to tell Ruth, but not now, not until all the plans had been talked about between her and Isaac.

Ruth leaned in close. "What have you done, Molly?"

Isaac reappeared through the shop's door before Molly could explain herself. He used one hand to manipulate a small bike inside. He wore a smile, but was silent, almost broody.

Ruth lifted her head and sniffed. "Is that pizza I smell?" She sat forward and scooted to the edge of the couch. "How about we all go get something to eat? I can take the leftovers home to Saul." She grabbed her purse and headed for the door.

"You ladies go. Enjoy. I've got work to do. *Danke* for helping out." Isaac walked toward the desk, his limp more pronounced. Molly watched as he carefully sat, then swung around the computer chair, his face a chalky white.

The smile on his face looked forced to Molly. As she shut the shop door, she noticed his hand go to his injured leg and rub. He was in pain. *Poor man.*

Disappointment and relief battled within her as she trailed behind Ruth toward the pizza shop. She wanted Isaac to come with them, but was glad he didn't. The agreement between them had left her tense, unsettled. She should have kept her mouth shut and not told Ruth about her and Isaac's deception. What if Ruth couldn't be trusted? She could tell someone, and the truth could get back to *Mamm.*

Amish women loved to gossip. It was something to help pass the hours as they quilted, a tasty tidbit they could share over their fences. They were all the same. Ruth was no exception. Still, she and Isaac would only be pretending for a few weeks and then would part as friends. No one would be hurt by their little deception.

The smell of hot pizza floated into his bike shop, causing Isaac's stomach to growl in loud protest. He had to count his pennies after the bicycle debacle at the thrift store. He glanced over at the six dented bikes lined up at the back of the store. At half price, the cost of the bikes had still taken a huge bite out of his food money. He'd have to tighten his belt. Miss a few dinners until he sold something.

The bell rang out. Isaac glanced toward the door. Molly came charging in, her cheeks a rosy pink. She handed over a small, square pizza box and grinned awkwardly. "Ruth and I couldn't eat the whole pie. I thought you might enjoy the last three slices while you work."

Isaac took the box from her hand. "*Danke*, but I thought Ruth was taking home the leftovers to her husband."

Molly's smile disappeared and a grooved frown replaced it.

"*Ya*, she was." She fingered her prayer *kapp* ribbons. Her voice rose an octave, just enough to let him know she was uncomfortable. "She changed her mind...well, not exactly changed her mind. I might have mentioned that you were probably hungry."

He placed the pizza box on his desk and then turned back toward her. "You didn't have to take care of me, Molly. I have some peanut butter crackers in my desk drawer reserved for busy days like this."

"Oh. I didn't know." She glanced toward the shop door, edging away, inch by inch. A red flush creeped up her neck. "I'll see you later then. Tonight. At dinner. *Mamm*'s making fried chicken." She almost smiled. "We have the singing at seven if you're still willing to come."

"*Ya*, I want to come." He did want to go with her and wished he didn't. They were just starting their courting charade, and already he regretted it. He shouldn't be taking the chance of falling in love with Molly. When she found out the truth about him, she'd back away, leave him brokenhearted.

She fumbled for the doorknob behind her. "*Gut*. I'm glad. Well…enjoy your pizza."

"Sure," he said, leaning against the low wall to take the weight off his aching leg.

The bell over the door rang wildly as Molly rushed out and down the sidewalk, leaving Isaac alone with his thoughts.

Isaac knew very little about women, but he

recognized infatuation when he saw it. Molly had waited a long time to find love, but he was the wrong man for her. Somehow he had to make sure she saw that without crushing her young heart.

Chapter Six

"Don't break that," Ulla urged, her brow arched in annoyance.

Molly glanced at her *mamm*'s expression of disapproval, slowed her pace and then placed her *grossmammi*'s beloved chicken platter gently on the linen-covered dining room table.

She pushed a golden brown, perfectly fried chicken leg away from the plate's edge and then turned to head back to the kitchen.

"It makes me to wonder what all the rush is about," her *mamm* said in a low tone, straightening first Isaac's dinner plate and then stabbing a small knife into the dish of homemade butter.

Molly watched as Isaac meandered through the dining room door and joined them, his dark hair still damp from a shower and curling at the ends.

"This looks *gut*," he said, and pulled out the chair he'd been assigned to by Ulla's gesture. Molly smiled blandly at him. Ulla ignored him completely.

"*Danke*, Isaac. *Mamm* knows her way around a frying pan," Molly said, cutting a glance at her mother who was busy placing knives and forks next to three perfectly spaced plates.

Molly frowned, and fluttered her eyelashes as a warning to Isaac. Her mother didn't acknowledge Isaac coming into the room or Molly's compliment in any way. The older woman was still stewing in some kind of silent simmer, having declared she'd had a long day when she'd begun to cook an hour earlier. Ulla remained silent as Molly assisted in any way she could.

Molly breathed in deeply. She'd had a long day, too, and the last thing she needed was to be treated like some careless schoolgirl by her sullen mother.

Isaac's gaze flicked from Molly to Ulla, as if gauging the temperature between the two women.

Molly left Isaac to fend for himself. He was a grown man. Let him deal with her *mamm*'s bad mood for a few moments. She had other things to do. There was creamed corn to place on the table before they could eat, and it was already close to six.

In her haste she almost dropped the bowl of corn, and moments later she dripped a trail of water as she filled three glasses at the table. The singing frolic began promptly at seven. The Mennonite sports field would fill up quickly. It always did. She and Isaac would have to hurry if they wanted to find a good spot before the singing began.

"You have somewhere to be, *dochder*? A child to birth? A shift at the café?" Ulla lowered herself into her chair, scooted forward and then clasped her hands in her ample lap.

Molly had hoped they could get through the meal before telling her *mamm* she and Isaac were going out together. There'd be words, and in the black mood her mother was in, they'd probably be harsh and embarrassing. It was inevitable. "The frolic is at seven." She hadn't lied. She just hadn't said she and Isaac would be going together and begin their courting ruse.

They prayed in silence and then Ulla's prayer *kapp* fluttered as she turned her head and took in Isaac's freshly pressed dress shirt and clean trousers. "Will you be going to this frolic, Herr Graber?"

Isaac pulled his hand back from the table. "*Ya*, I thought I would."

"I see," Ulla said, fingering the edge of her plate. Her gaze shifted to Molly, to the clean dress she'd changed into just before they sat down to eat. Her mouth formed a hard edge.

"Will you two be going together?"

Molly bristled, realizing after tonight there would be plenty of questions to answer, but they didn't have to be answered now. Her *mamm* would be furious when she thought Molly had shoved Samuel aside for Isaac, a man who had no money.

Isaac nodded as he shoveled the last of his peas into his mouth and chewed vigorously. "I thought you'd think it best." He glanced up, his expression innocent. "We can't have you worrying that I might fall again."

Ulla smiled. "*Ya*, sure. That's fine. And will Samuel be coming, Molly?"

"*Ya*, he usually shows up if there's food at the frolic."

"*Gut,*" Ulla said with a nod, letting her daughter's comment about Samuel's robust appetite slide past. She stopped to take a sip of water, then turned back to Molly. "Don't worry about the dishes tonight, *dochder.* I'll do them.

You two best hurry now. You'll want a good spot up front."

Molly didn't need to be told twice. *"Danke, Mamm."* She slipped from her chair and darted toward the kitchen, her relief visible on her smiling face. "Hurry, Isaac. I'll grab the cookies. You grab the quilt."

"Is the frolic being held at your church?" Isaac asked ten minutes later as Molly sped through the sun-filled streets, the cart puttering along at a good clip.

"Nee. Not this time." She turned down a short street and joined a group of Amish bike riders. She slowed, waving to several women her own age as they passed. "The Mennonite church is sponsoring the community frolic. Most of the singings are held during the busy part of the winter. It's not so hot, and there's a lot more *youngies* looking for something to do."

"You're sure about starting the ruse tonight?" Isaac asked.

"You heard *Mamm.* 'Is Samuel going to be there?' She's still pushing him in my face. If it's to stop, I have to take a stand."

"I just thought…"

Molly parked the golf cart next to the church's chain-link fence and then turned to Isaac. "Are you backing out, because if you are, I understand." She checked the position of her *kapp* and then picked up the cookies and slid out of the cart. "I'm not comfortable about lying, either, even for a little while. I just don't know what else to do."

Daylight didn't seem to be in any hurry to fade away. Molly looked Isaac's way but couldn't read his undecipherable expression. She did hear the tone in his voice as he said, "I'm your friend, Molly. I'll do what I can to help you out. You know that."

She extended her hand his way.

Isaac looked her in the eyes, seemed to momentarily hesitate, but then grabbed her hand and pulled her toward the growing crowd arriving around them. "Let's get this mess with Samuel Bawell settled, once and for all."

She liked the feel of his rough palm pressed against hers, the way his warm fingers intertwined around hers. A thrill shot through her, and she was surprised by the power of it. She glanced up at Isaac as they walked, tethered to him in a way that made her heart beat fast and wild. But all this wasn't real. He wasn't walking out with her, wasn't her true love. He was just a man who felt he owed her a favor and was paying her back in a kind way. Her joy died a silent death. Her smile faded. Once Samuel went back home, Isaac would step away.

Isn't that what she wanted? Her independence? Molly wasn't quite sure.

Isaac hobbled to a distant bench at the back of the baseball field and sat alone, his cane leaning against his leg. The volleyball game was going well, the *youngies*' enthusiasm growing as Molly launched the ball across the net again and again, winning points for her Amish teammates.

Memories came back to haunt him. Thomas had been playing the same game the day he died. They'd all yelled themselves hoarse encouraging their team. Thomas had twisted his ankle playing this game. It was the reason Isaac had been driving the old truck on the country road back to his Mennonite friend's farm.

A spasm of pain clutched his thigh, reminding him he hadn't died in the crash. So why did he feel so dead inside?

Two laughing Mennonite girls ran past and waved. Dressed less formally than Molly's pale blue dress and starched white *kapp*, they wore simple but bright colored dresses, with no *kapps*, their hair pulled back into long ponytails that streamed behind them. They ran barefoot across the soft grass.

He waved back at them, but didn't smile. He didn't feel like smiling. He felt like sobbing out his heart for Thomas right there on the bench.

Isaac looked up to see Molly's wild ball shoot over the net and win the game for her Amish team. The game ended suddenly, with a choir of shouts. She came running toward him, glowing with excitement.

"Did you see my last serve? I thought I'd completely missed the ball, but then it caught the edge of my fist and went soaring past them all." She plopped down next to him and grabbed him around the neck, her arms hugging him tight to her side. She smelled of fresh air and lilacs. He gently pulled her arms from his neck and shifted away an inch or two. "I'm proud of you. I really am."

Molly's laughter stopped. She scooted away, putting more distance between them. Isaac had a smile on his face, but it didn't reach his eyes. Her closeness had made him uncomfortable. "I'm sorry I got caught up in the moment. Forgive me for overstepping my boundaries."

"Don't be silly. We're supposed to be pretending to be courting. No harm done." A breeze picked up. He pulled his straw hat down, his green eyes avoiding hers.

Then why did he look so uncomfortable? "It's getting dark. The singing should begin in a moment. You coming?"

"*Ya*, sure. I don't want to miss all the fun." This time he held out his hand to her.

She placed her hand in his and did her best to ignore the electricity that ran through her fingers as they walked across the field, him limping and her slowing her pace to match his steps.

"Most people sit in the bleachers, but we can use the quilt and sit on the ground if you'd prefer."

"*Nee*, the bleachers are fine," Isaac said, taking the lead, their hands still clasped, weaving them in and out of people until he found a spot big enough for the two of them on the first row.

Wedged in on both sides, Molly had never sat so close to Isaac before, but he didn't seem concerned about their proximity now. He grinned down at her and then gave all his attention to the singers who clustered together and began an old worship song Molly remembered from her younger years. The song was fast and lively, causing her to tap her foot as she'd done as a child.

Movement from the corner of her eye caught

her attention. Samuel walked past, his eyes flicking over Isaac and then her. Unsmiling, he tipped his dark hat her way and then proceeded on.

"Was that Samuel?" Isaac inquired.

"*Ya*," she responded and witnessed the instant change in Isaac's expression, felt the tension in his hand she still held. It took every ounce of willpower she possessed to remain still and calm. The expression Samuel threw her way spoke volumes. Samuel would tell her *mamm* that she and Isaac were setting close, holding hands.

There was the lie to tell her *mamm* about her and Isaac's courtship and then the questions she'd be asked. Her *mamm* would be disappointed in her, make a fuss. How would her mother treat Isaac once she had heard? Would she ask him to leave their home?

The tempo of the music became soft, the words to the old Amish song tugging at her heart. The words said *Gott* would sustain them, keep them strong in the Lord. Had she angered *Gott* with her plan? Would her lie distance her from Him, from His salvation?

She watched as Isaac rubbed at his leg, his brow creasing into deep furrows. "Is your leg troubling you?"

He looked down, pale, his mouth a fixed line. "Some."

"We can go now if you want."

"*Nee*, you said you wanted to hear the singing. I'll be fine."

Molly rose and tugged at his arm. "Come on. The singing will go on until ten. Let's go home."

He stood and had to brace himself against his cane for the first time that day.

They moved toward the parking lot, their steps slow, Isaac holding on to his cane for support.

"I'm sorry, Isaac. I didn't think of the long walk to the bleachers. I should have suggested we go somewhere less strenuous because of your leg," Molly said as they reached the golf cart.

He slid into the passenger seat. "I'm fine. The doctor said I should be venturing out more now, putting more weight on my leg."

Molly started the engine and turned on the cart's lights. "I think we should talk about this courtship, Isaac. I hadn't thought about how my *mamm* might act toward you once we began the ruse." She reached out and touched his arm. "It could get ugly. She might even ask you to leave the house."

"You let me worry about your *mamm*. Your job is to look happy and smile a lot."

She drove away from the church, the little golf cart sputtering in protest as she gunned it. "I had a good time tonight," she said, glancing at him. She saw him grasp the edge of the cart and hold on. Molly knew she did many things well, but driving wasn't one of them.

"So did I. We'll have to do something else later this week if you're free. I heard there's a pie-eating contest coming up soon, and a public auction I'd like to go to if you're interested."

Molly sped down the well-lit street, her thoughts a jumbled mess. The words to the old hymn came back to haunt her. *Gott will take care of you.* She longed to have this charade over, but knew she'd miss Isaac more than she wanted to admit when he walked away.

Chapter Seven

Dressed in dark trousers and a fresh white shirt and matching vest, his cane polished to a honey glow, Isaac gave the Old Order Amish church a glance and favored his healing but still throbbing leg as he slowly rode past the brick building on his bicycle. A row of traditionally dressed Amish men stood at the side doors of the building, their line ending on the grassy lawn.

He leaned toward the more modern Anabaptist church philosophy, not that he ignored Ordnung rules or bylaws of the church. One of the many reasons he'd decided to come to Pinecraft was to get away from his disappointed, angry, Old Order Amish father. The man ran his home with harsh rules that felt more manmade than *Gott*-given since Thomas's death.

Isaac rode on. When he'd arrived in Pine-craft, he'd been surprised to hear the community had built churches, their houses too small to accommodate local church services during peak seasons.

With the turn of his bike handles, he pulled into the driveway of the smaller New Order Amish church a few streets over and headed to the back parking lot. A line of six young, unmarried men stood behind a stretch of older men with long beards blowing in the wind. Some nodded in his direction as he parked his bike and hobbled up. Several were stone-faced as his father had always been on Sundays before church, but most smiled a greeting.

Isaac glanced around, saw a few familiar faces, but Molly was nowhere in sight. They hadn't agreed to meet at church when they'd gone their separate ways the night before. She'd gone to her room without a glance back, and he'd avoided the kitchen when he'd left early that morning in hopes of avoiding Ulla.

Several of the elders filed into the church through the building's side door. Isaac recognized Mose, and his father, Bishop Otto Fischer.

A line of married men went into the church. He entered with the single men. He was pleasantly surprised to see the church had been well cared for and freshly painted.

He took his seat and positioned his leg for comfort. He knew the three-hour service was going to be taxing, but he'd made a promise to *Gott* about being an active member of this new church, and he was going to keep that promise.

Opening prayers were said. Mose Fischer sang a hymn, his voice a rich baritone. He led the congregation in several songs, some Isaac knew from his home church services and some new to him. Peace calmed his troubled soul. He sang with all his heart, his love for *Gott* deepening as he took in the words of salvation. *Gott*'s promise of hope and forgiveness reached him, the needed words preached by a zealous pastor whose youthful voice still broke at times.

Gott spoke to Isaac's heart, revealed His promise of forgiveness for all who would ask. The pain of his bottled-up grief and guilt eased some. Perhaps his Father's love for him had remained strong, even though Thomas was dead.

A child began to cry, drawing Isaac's attention to the women's side of the church. Molly sat beside a red-haired woman who held a small *bobbel* in her arms.

He caught Molly's eye and nodded. She nodded back, a quick smile playing on her lips, but then she turned back toward the singer standing at the front of the church.

Three hours later his leg hurt like stinging ants and his stomach rumbled, reminding him he'd missed breakfast. He needed to move around, get the blood flowing back in his leg. He also needed to eat. Living off two meals a day was hard on a man, especially one with his big appetite.

When he had entered the church, he had noticed signs for the church-wide meal Molly had mentioned the night before. The food would be served on the grounds at Pinecraft Park directly after the service. The thought of good homemade Amish food had his mouth watering as he headed out the door into the bright Florida sunshine. Maybe he'd get a chance to talk to Molly if he hurried.

Two containers of hot food fit in Molly's bike basket, with just enough room for condiments and dessert. She pedaled as fast as she could, but a combination of cars and bikes whizzed past, forcing her onto the graveled verge for the last mile. Hopping off the bike and pushing it through the grass, she looked around for her mother and found Samuel Bawell waiting for her at the end of a row of long plastic tables.

Women with hungry husbands bustled around, quickly covering the tables with white tablecloths.

Samuel frowned into the sun as she approached, his rich brown eyes looking her up and down. He wore a blue shirt of fine cotton fabric, his dark suspenders holding up well pressed and creased dark trousers.

A gust of wind blew off his straw hat, exposing his mussed mahogany-colored hair cut bowl-shaped around his ears.

"Here, let me help you," he offered, and began to unload her basket, wanting to make points with her no doubt and squelch any possible rumors of her and Isaac's budding courtship.

She avoided giving him a side hug of thanks, as was the custom for non-courting couples that were looking for mates—not that she would want Samuel as a future husband, or any other man for that matter. Samuel was her mother's idea of the perfect Amish man. Not hers. His controlling nature and self-importance irritated Molly beyond words.

Every time she saw him, he pushed for a commitment from her. Just because she was twenty-one years old and a spinster didn't mean she had to throw herself at the first man who asked her to marry him.

Samuel grabbed her hands, held her gaze. His dimpled smile should have set her heart to racing, but it didn't.

She sighed, hearing her mother's rasping voice in her head. *You need to make a good marriage so I can end my days in comfort, Molly.*

Everyone knew the Bawell family had big money—a lot more than most Amish families who came to Pinecraft for the winter. Their large farm prospered, the rich Ohio soil yielding big crops that added to their wealth yearly.

Samuel made sure everyone heard about their success each winter. He was proud of the farm and how successful the family had become after leaving the dry dirt of Lancaster County. Molly wasn't impressed and prayed *Gott* would speak to him about sharing more with his community and talking less about his prosperity.

His thumb rubbed her hand as he spoke. "I missed you."

"You just saw me last night at the singing." Molly pulled her hands away. She took a plastic container of whoopie pies from her basket and placed them on the table. Samuel groaned, a hopeful smile playing on his lips as he recognized the container of mouth-watering desserts. "Did you make red velvet this time?"

With a nod Molly continued to unpack. The first wave of men lined up at the head table. She had to hurry.

Busy watching Molly, Samuel almost spilled a covered plate of fried chicken. He performed an impressive balancing act, recovering cleverly. He bowed at the waist, impressed with himself. "Have I told you how sweet you look today?"

"*Nee.* I've told you repeatedly that compliments embarrass me. I'm not a vain person, Samuel. I don't need to be told when my hair shines or my eyes sparkle." Knowing she was being harsh, she put her head down as she took the pickle relish out of her bike basket and then grabbed for a large pickle jar full of hot celery soup that needed to be poured into her mother's old tureen.

"*Ya*, sure. I'll try to remember. No more compliments." Samuel rushed around the table and poured the soup for her, smiling, trying to be helpful.

Molly shrugged, her stomach roiling. She had to explain to him about her and Isaac and finalize the lie about their courting. Her words would confirm Samuel's suspicions and make him furious, but they would hold back his advances and send him home to Ohio single.

Maybe one day she'd be ready for marriage, but never to Samuel.

"I saw you with that cripple last night," Samuel said, handing her a container of chocolate-chip cookies for the children.

"That's cruel, even from you, Samuel." She turned her back on him.

Several servers showed up, stopping Molly and Samuel's conversation, but she knew he'd have more to say. He always did.

"I'll find us a spot under our tree." Samuel walked past her and began filling his plate with most of the crispy fried chicken she'd brought and a huge mound of hot potato salad. He headed for the shaded area where the *youngies* gathered during outdoor meals. Molly watched him walk away, his stride long and confident. He was handsome, but his good looks hid a dark side she wanted to avoid at all costs.

Molly welcomed her mother and several friends as they approached the tables.

"Where's Samuel?" Ulla asked, setting down a huge platter of potato pancakes covered in waxed paper. The older woman wiped sweat from her face with the hem of her apron.

"Somewhere with the singles, I guess." Molly moved the pancakes over, removed the covering and added a fork for serving.

"You should go join him, take him a plate of food."

"*Ach*, he's got plenty to eat. He's a real *wutz*."

"So the man likes his food. That doesn't make him a pig. Did you talk to him, serve him yourself?"

"*Ya*. We talked for a few moments." A strong gust of wind ruffled her hair, pulling strands from her bun and tickling her neck. "He seemed in a hurry to eat and rushed off."

"Join him. Let him know you're interested in being beside him. You'll never catch a husband like this, Molly." Her mother leaned in close. "Remember what I told you. We're getting fewer and fewer renters each year. Soon we'll be alone in that big house, just you and me…with little money coming in and a burden on our community. A good marriage would end all that." Ulla's eyes narrowed as she hissed, "Go on. Show him what a catch you are."

This seemed the perfect time to tell her mother she meant it when she said she had no interest in Samuel, but people mingled around them, gathering food, making small talk.

Molly filled a plate for herself and walked

away, leaving her mother to believe she was being an obedient daughter. But she had no intention of finding Samuel. A solitary meal near the river appealed to her more. She'd worked hard all week at the café and delivered two babies, both late at night, the births cutting deep into her sleep. Tired in body and spirit, she longed for a place to contemplate all the wonderful nature around her and leave her stress behind.

Isaac's boots dug into the soft sandy dirt as he gathered a plate of food and made his way across the small park, leaving the swarm of chattering people behind. He was in no mood for idle chitchat. The sermon had stirred his heart, put a grain of hope in his heart for the future. He had a lot to think about. It didn't matter where he ate, as long as it was quiet and peaceful. Over the course of the past few months, he'd grown used to eating alone.

Clusters of young orange trees grew all around the park. An old picnic table called to him, and he headed toward it.

Setting his plate on the warped wood, he took a seat, glad to be off his aching leg. True to the doctor's words, his bones were mending, his leg hurting less and less, but the way he was forced to walk hadn't changed. He'd live with the noticeable limp in his stride forever. He knew he deserved nothing more.

He prayed silently over his food, grateful for the chance to eat and not worry how he'd pay for his next meal. His savings spent, *Gott*'s mercy and love surrounded him as he whispered his appreciation for this bounty provided today and the fresh, growing peace in his heart.

Isaac lifted his head and began to eat, shoveling in food as fast as he could chew. For days his lunches had consisted of nothing more than crackers and peanut butter. Ulla had warned him she'd start charging extra for evening meals. This free Amish food tasted like manna from heaven.

"You miss breakfast?" Molly meandered up the slight grassy incline, her plate in hand. A cool breeze tilted her white *kapp*, leaving it at comical angle.

"*Ya*, I did. *Willkumm*. Share my table." Isaac motioned for her to join him. He brushed leaves off the table and watched her hesitate only a moment before sitting on the other side of the wooden bench.

Her presence was a breath of fresh air, a joy to his senses. He longed to share his newfound appreciation and love for *Gott*, but sharing meant explaining why he'd run away from

Missouri, why his life was broken into pieces. Perhaps he'd tell her about Thomas's death one day, but he wasn't prepared to share the raw pain today. Not even for Molly.

"Danke," Molly murmured, and began to nibble at her food.

"I'm surprised you're not with your friends." Isaac stuffed a round whoopie pie into his mouth. He struggled to politely chew the enormous mouthful. The red velvet cake was as light as a feather and moist, better than any he'd ever eaten. He grinned at her and stuffed in another small pie. "I'm going to marry whoever made these," he teased, and reached for the last pie on his plate.

"You'll be marrying me for real then," Molly said, giggling like a young girl.

He set down the last of the round cake. "I had no idea…" Isaac coughed.

For the moment Molly seemed to be enjoying his discomfort. Her smile was wide and easygoing. "Oh, now he tries to *rutsch* his way out of a fine proposal," she said to the wind, her smile growing as his embarrassment increased.

"Nee, I didn't mean to suggest…"

Molly forked a tiny red potato and held it near her mouth. "What? Suggest we really court, get wed this Christmas season?"

"I was just saying how delicious this whoopie pie tasted. My remark was meant only as a joke. Something to laugh at." He felt his face grow warm. He prayed he wasn't blushing like a foolish *youngie*.

"It wonders me. Are you saying you *don't* want to marry me for real, Isaac Graber? That I'm not good enough for you?" Molly's expression had been playful and relaxed, but now she looked serious, her brow furrowed, her mouth a firm, angry line.

At first he'd enjoyed the idea of pretending to be Molly's future husband, but now her teasing conversation awakened new thoughts in his mind. What if she had taken his comments seriously? He hadn't meant to make her believe he was truly interested in her, in a real courtship.

They had no future together.

Pain pierced his knee. He'd never forgive himself for what he'd done to Thomas, even if *Gott* forgave him. His newfound joy evaporated. He cleared his throat and spoke without humor. "What I meant to say was, you're a wonderful cook."

Cleanup was always the worst part of church picnics, especially if the person cleaning up was in a bad mood of her own making.

Molly pulled a big plastic trash can over to the table and began disposing of leftover food, banging plastic containers against the soft side of the plastic-lined trash container. Deep in thought, she ignored the shadow falling across her face and kept working.

"I thought we were going to eat together," Samuel said, his brow arched in an angry scowl. "I looked everywhere for you. Where'd you disappear to?"

Molly stilled, the pot she'd been scraping forgotten. Samuel stood in front of her, his hands planted on his hips, a frown on his sunburned face. Behind him the sinking sun created spikes of pale reds and yellows behind wispy gray clouds.

This is not the time to push me, Samuel Bawell.

Her attention wandered back to the pot in her hand. "I never told you I was joining you." A stubborn glop of burned cheese refused to budge. Her temper flared. She exchanged her spoon for a dull knife and scraped as if her life depended on removing the gluey food.

"You didn't answer my question. Where did you go? To find that cripple, Isaac Graber?"

"That's my business, Samuel. Not yours." Her eyes cut in his direction, narrowed, angry.

Words were about to be unleashed, and he wouldn't like them.

"This is no way for a courting woman to act, Molly. I know you're inexperienced, but…" He took a step around the table and reached for her hand.

Molly inhaled a deep, cleansing breath and forced it out again. It was time he understood where they stood. "We are *not* courting. I keep telling you over and over again, but you don't like what you hear so you refuse to listen. We are just friends. We have gone to a few volleyball games and attended church singings. Nothing more. I am *not* your girl."

"But your *mamm* said you were interested, that we could be wed in the church by the end of this year."

A tide of fury washed over her. "I'm sorry. My *mamm* was wrong to tell you I was ready for marriage. I'm not interested in you that way, Samuel. You're not my type."

"But Isaac Graber is?"

"My mother doesn't own me, nor can she decide who I marry. This talk of courtship and marriage has to end now."

Somewhere close by, a seagull shrieked a warning and Molly glanced up, watching Samuel.

He flushed red. His gaze dropped. "You'll be sorry you turned me down someday. You'll see. But I won't bother you again, Molly." No dimples appeared on his cheeks as he turned on his heel and walked away, his broad shoulders squared, his gait fast.

Her thoughts scrambled. The idea of hurting anyone wounded her soul, but it had to be done. She had to have a serious conversation with her *mamm*. These embarrassing situations had to stop. Why wouldn't she let her live her own life, make her own choices? Everyone in Pinecraft seemed to know all her business, think it was their job to give her advice, and she was tired of it. She would have to go through with the farce she'd planned with Isaac if she was to find peace. She had no other choice.

She scrubbed with renewed vigor until the pot's bottom was spotless. Something drew her eye, and she watched as Isaac hobbled across the grass toward the walkway, his dark hat pulled low on his head. He spoke to no one as people passed.

She grabbed a pan and began to fight the dried-on food, thinking back to Isaac's expression when he'd told her what a wonderful cook she was, but in the same breath proclaimed his lack of real interest in her.

A refreshing wind blew, ruffling the loose hairs on her sweaty neck and cooling her. She silently prayed as she finished emptying the last of the dishes and pans, asking forgiveness from *Gott* for her show of temper.

People passed, spoke and strolled away. Men assigned to help the ladies fold away tables and carry dishes finally showed up full of conversation about the awesome domino gamed they'd played.

"*Ya*, I would have won if I hadn't used that double ten when I did." Chicken John Schwarts, one of Pinecraft's favorite pranksters, cackled like one of the hens he raised on his farm just outside Sarasota. The thin, frail man had gained her mother's interest the past few weeks, and they had begun to court. But with their growing money problems, and Molly's refusal to marry, she knew her mother was probably leading the wealthy man on in hopes of a profitable marriage. If he didn't propose soon, her *mamm* would drop him, leave him with a broken heart and look for another man with money. Not that their financial problems were so dire. If her *mamm* would stop spending foolishly, they could make ends meet, pay all the bills beginning to pile up.

Chicken John lifted a box filled with plastic food containers that belonged to the church and the bottom fell out. Dirty containers scattered in the ankle-high grass. Everyone laughed, enjoying the scene of the little man on his knees, scurrying around picking up lids and containers. But Molly remained somber, her heart heavy. She carried two lightweight boxes to the golf carts lined up as transport back to the church. There'd be dishes to wash and put away. She looked forward to the hard work. Her mind would be too busy to think about what she'd said to Samuel and what he'd said back to her.

Would she regret turning him down? She glanced at her built-up shoe. Isaac was temporarily disabled, and it was evident he didn't want her as a *frau*. He needed someone strong to help build his bike shop into the success he dreamed of. There were plenty of young girls looking for someone to court and wed. Someone would catch his eye one day soon.

She threw her leg over her bike and began to pedal. So what if she'd have to live her life single and alone? It was better than marrying without love. The image of Isaac walking alone across the park came back to haunt her. Did he feel lonely, too?

Chapter Eight

Isaac woke from a restless night, his breathing labored and his hair damp with sweat. The recurring nightmare that disturbed his sleep still tormented him.

He had been driving. Headlights sped toward him. He fought to swerve, his fingers gripped the truck's steering wheel until his knuckles turned white. But the crash still came. The sound of metal tearing metal cut through his brain. Pain was everywhere. Thomas lay on the ground. Isaac stifled a shout and pulled himself out of the black fog.

With the back of his hand, he wiped sweat off his brow and threw back the covers, the ache in his leg forcing him to slowly maneuver out of the bed. He limped to the window.

Somewhere in the house Molly sang a familiar worship song, her voice sweet and low.

He had wanted to get out of the house early this morning, before she woke and started her day. He needed time to think about their pretend courtship. He owed her a big favor, but it wasn't like him to break form and lie. He didn't think it was Molly's way, either.

What if they fell in love after spending time together? Stranger things had happened. They could never have a future together. Not after the choices he had made. When she found out about the accident, Thomas's death...she wouldn't want him. He had to face that there may never be a real courting or marriage for him. He didn't deserve the joy of being a husband and father.

He ran his hands though his hair, his frustration growing. He knew so little about *Englischer* laws. Would he go to prison if the *Englischer* police found out he'd been driving Thomas's truck that night?

The Amish had their own laws and ways of handling legal situations. The power of his community, the rules his bishop laid down, was all Isaac knew. When his *daed* directed him to speak up to the bishop and elders, he'd confessed his sin to them. They'd prayed for his forgiveness from *Gott*. Wasn't that how he'd always done things? Hold firm to his Amish ways? So why was he still feeling so guilty? Would he ever feel forgiven, be able to live a normal life?

He had no money, no home. There was only his business, and it might never be a money-maker. He lived hand-to-mouth and wasn't about to ask any woman to live that way, too.

Especially Molly.

He quickly showered, dressed and sneaked out the kitchen door, his hair still wet, his cane in hand. The pavement was damp from an early-morning rain shower. He wiped down the seat of his golf cart and backed out of the driveway, not looking back.

Molly's hand smoothed out the crumpled quilt and then punched her pillows into fluffy mounds. She'd slept poorly, her eyes stinging with grit from too little sleep after spending two hours of her night with a first-time mother's false alarm. Outside her window Isaac's new golf cart started up. She turned from her bed, her attention pulled toward the noise of the cart engine. She pulled back her bedroom curtain and watched as he drove down the drive and onto the street, headed toward town.

"Ach!" She'd wanted to talk to him while her *mamm* wasn't around. They had to come to a clear understanding before she spoke to her mother.

Glad for a day off from the café, she began to ready the rooms for guests coming the next day. The kitchen always took the longest to clean and required the most work. She started by cleaning the oven and then wiped down all the wooden cabinets with linseed oil and a soft cloth.

"You look busy," Ulla said, coming through the back door a few moments later. She flung a thrift-store bag in the middle of the kitchen table.

"Was tut Sie bier?" Molly asked, glancing at the store bag and then her *mamm*. She flashed her a scowl. The table had been freshly scrubbed a moment before, and now it would need to be cleaned again.

Ulla pulled out a pair of cutoff jeans and a large man's T-shirt from one of the bags and held the trousers up against her body, muttering unintelligible words that clearly had something to do with them possibly not fitting her ample hips. Ulla glanced up. "I live here, *bensel.* Where else would I be?"

"I thought you were spending the day fishing with Chicken John." Molly smirked as her *mamm* winced at the man's community nickname. Ulla flushed rosy pink, something Molly hadn't seen her do in a long time.

"I've told you before. Stop calling him that, especially to his face. There's nothing wrong with him owning a chicken farm. It's a respectable occupation, and you like eating the eggs his chickens lay well enough." Ulla reached for a glass from the overhead cabinet next to the sink and turned on the tap.

Molly couldn't help but notice her *mamm*'s flush had crept all the way down to her neck when she turned around to scold her.

"Are you stringing Chicken John along for his money?"

"What a thing to say to your *mamm*. Of course I'm not. I truly like him. He's good to me, and kind spirited." Ulla took a sip of water and then added, "I know you'll probably find this hard to believe, but he seems to like me, too."

"Is there an announcement coming soon?" Molly almost laughed out loud when her *mamm* swallowed down the wrong pipe and sputtered. "You've gotten very rude since you began working at that café. Perhaps it's time I pay a visit and speak to your boss about manners."

A mental image of her mother and Willa Mae going toe-to-toe in front of a café full of gossipy customers put a grin back on her face. "That's a good idea. Maybe you could bring Chicken John with you and then have a meal on me."

"*Ya*, a real smart-mouth, just as I said, and in *mei haus*. I've known John for years. He's been like a *bruder* to me. There's nothing more to say." Ulla snatched her bags off the table and stomped past, her bedroom door slamming with a resounding *bang* a few seconds later.

Molly smiled as she hurried to answer the front doorbell.

His bowl-cut gray hair shoved under a navy blue baseball cap, Chicken John stood on the doorstep, his small body swallowed up by a checked, long-sleeved fishing shirt. Pale, skinny legs protruded from his baggy work pants rolled all the way to his knobby knees.

Molly held back a titter of laughter. "Looks like you're ready for a sunny day of fishing."

"*Ya*. Seems your *mamm* has no intentions of coming home until we catch our dinner." He grinned and then glanced around Molly. "Your *mamm*'s not ready yet?"

"She's dressing now. Would you like to come in?"

"*Nee*, not like this." He looked down at

his worn fishing boots covered in sand and shrugged. "I smell of fish bait and the old boat. Maybe next time."

Dressed in a plain dress, with jeans that covered her legs, Ulla rushed past Molly, her tennis shoes squeaking on the hardwood floors as she headed toward the door. "It makes me to wonder why you've become so foolhardy of late, Molly. Perhaps there's more for us to talk about when I get home."

Molly shut the door and leaned against it.

Had Samuel told her *mamm* about her commitment to Isaac?

Isaac rang up the inexpensive tire valve and forced a smile on his face as he handed back the change from his customer's dollar bill. "*Danke.* Come back to see us," he said, and watched the burly teenager walk out the door. The boy had come in for two new bike tires, but he didn't have the right size in stock for one. Another sale lost.

He looked down at the dollar bill in his hand. Should he add it to the two quarters, two dimes, a nickel and four pennies in the money drawer? Not even enough to buy his lunch. He folded the money and dropped it in his pocket and then wrote the sale down in his book under the correct date. At this rate he wouldn't be able to pay for new supplies at the end of the month, much less his rent to Ulla, even if she let him stay after she heard the news of his courting her daughter. Where would he go to live?

Silence ate at him. He could hear the low hum of a dryer going around and around at the Laundromat next door. He'd had no business for hours, yet there was always a line out its door, Amish and *Englischer* snowbirds waiting for fresh clothes during peak season. Maybe he'd gone into the wrong business. Maybe he should go back to Missouri, face his family's disappointment and the police with the truth.

Isaac sat on the red couch and watched traffic go by. He perked up in his seat and stretched to watch as Molly flew past his window, pedaling her bike like time was against her. Her medical bag bounced in the wire basket behind her seat. Another baby to be birthed by the everbusy woman. Her profession and work ethic warmed him. He'd never liked lazy people. There was nothing lazy about Molly Ziegler.

His stomach growled, but he ignored the call for food. He'd eat an apple in a bit and then wait for another inexpensive but delicious meal at home. *Home.* When had he started to think of Molly's house as his own? He'd lived there almost a month now. Even Ulla had warmed to him and treated him almost human at times. But would she treat him so well after she learned of them courting?

Isaac picked up a fashion magazine an *Englischer* had leafed through while waiting for a handlebar adjustment on her bike.

A thin *Englischer* woman in bright clothes that barely covered her body stared back at him. For a fleeting second he wondered what Molly would look like in a modest *Englischer* dress instead of the plain Amish clothes she wore.

An appealing image of her flashed through his mind. He sighed and started to toss the magazine in the trash, but caught a glimpse of an advertisement about bettering your business profits. He looked up the article's page number, turned to it and began to read. The writer was big on start-up loans for small businesses.

He thought about what he needed on the shelves, how a couple of extra rental carts could double, maybe triple his profit margin. He laid the magazine on the couch cushion next to him and leaned back, his eyes closed. Was he just being stubborn? Why not borrow a small loan from the church, just enough to get regular customers coming in?

Mose Fischer could help him make a decision. He was an elder in the modern Amish church they attended. Maybe he would be knowledgeable about loans and such. Isaac stood and stretched, his leg hurting, but not as much as it had in the past. The limp would remain, forever his companion.

Turning the Open sign over to Closed, he locked the main door and strolled toward the back exit. Excitement coursed through him. This loan idea could be the chance he needed to make his business thrive.

Tired but exhilarated after her patient's quick and easy birth of a healthy seven-pound boy, Molly returned home. She headed straight for Isaac's private room, a stack of fresh linens over one arm, her basket of cleaning supplies over the other.

She knocked on his door to make sure he hadn't come home early, then went in. Entering his room when he wasn't there felt strange. Her arm pimpled with goose bumps. She was being ridiculous. She'd cleaned his room a dozen times before.

She had a job to do and got busy working, a hum coming from the depth of her soul, calming her.

His bed was tidy but not properly made. *Typ-*

ical male. His curtains were closed so tightly not a beam of sunlight filtered in. Using both arms, she threw his drapes back and opened the two windows, allowing fresh air to blow into the small room. Rooms needed to breathe, her *mamm* had taught her as a small child. The scent of oak trees and sea breezes blew in, ruffling the curtains and flushing out the stale air.

She tore at his sheets and light quilt, and made a messy pile on the floor with the dirty linens. Leaving the mattress to air, she cleaned the windows with ammonia water and rubbed a shine into the glass windowpanes. A swipe of lemon water and baking soda cleaned the window ledges and doorknob. She grabbed a container of beeswax and went to work polishing the bed's headboard.

Moving over to his dresser, she lifted his Bible and couldn't resist the temptation to sniff the old leather-bound book. It reminded her of her *grossmammi*'s Bible from so long ago. As a child, she'd spent many hours in the Word, enjoying the pictures of the animals and people separating the pages of God's infinite words. Molly gave the old book a swipe of beeswax and then cleared the top of the dresser. She smeared a wax film all over the surface, hitting the sides and drawers for good measure.

When she was finished, the old dresser had a golden shine that would have impressed her *grossmammi* if she'd still been alive.

Prepared to remake the bed, Molly flipped out the clean bottom sheet, tucked in the corners and smoothed out any wrinkles left on the top sheet. She reached for the quilt on the chair and saw something white on the floor by the closet door. Almost ready to dust mop the room's wooden floors, she walked over and picked up an envelope, this one smaller than the ones she'd seen in his room before. It smelled of roses.

As the envelope was roughly opened, the name of the sender was partially torn. But Molly could make out the first name and the address clear enough. The name Rose, written in a small, feminine print, drew her attention. She turned the envelope over. Near the seal was a small X and the words *See you soon*.

She read the name Rose again and tapped the envelope against her hand as she pondered. Who was this Rose? His *mamm*? A sister? Maybe a cousin. She sniffed the envelope again. No *mamm* she knew would douse a letter to her son with sweet water. Perhaps he had a girlfriend back home?

Could he already be courting someone?

Maybe he'd agreed to her deception because he felt sorry for Molly?

Her face flamed. She often regretted her impulsive decision to ask him to fake a courtship. Maybe he did, too. Could she be causing him problems? She looked around for more letters on the floor, but only found dust bunnies under the bed.

Molly put the letter on the dresser and went back to making the bed, her thoughts lingering on the name Rose as she flipped the fresh quilt across the bed and punched air into Isaac's feather pillows. Whoever this Rose was, she lived in the same town Isaac had come from. Jamesport, Missouri.

She grabbed for the dust mop and began pushing it across the floor.

"I see you're still handy with the mop."

Molly flushed, remembering the bump she'd put on Isaac's head that first day. She glanced at the letter she'd just placed on the dresser and then leaned on the mop handle and sheepishly grinned his way. "*Ya*, the mop and I have become good friends." She tugged one of her *kapp*'s ribbons away from her face. "You're home early. No business?"

"Not much, but that could all change soon." He flashed a smile and then rested against the doorframe, his arms across his chest in a re-laxed manner. He seemed content to stand there and watch her finish the last of the cleaning. "I read an article in an *Englischer* magazine this afternoon."

"*Ya*, and what kind of advice did this maga-zine article suggest that puts such a big smile on your face?" Isaac seldom smiled like he meant it, and here he was smiling like the proverbial Cheshire cat over something *Englisch*. "I find hard work and perseverance usually pay off for me."

Isaac pulled off his straw hat and tapped it against his leg, his expression serious again. "*Ya*, well. I'm working hard at getting the busi-ness going, but if I don't have bikes to rent or parts to sell, it's tough meeting my customers' needs."

"You make a good point, but all businesses take time to get going."

"That's just it. I don't have the cash flow to wait for business to pick up. I need income now, and this article reminded me of something."

"And what is that?" Molly walked to the door, her mop and supplies in hand. She looked up into his green eyes and saw a fresh flash of fire smoldering there.

"I'm going to meet with Mose and see if I

can get a loan from the church. I just came home to clean up a bit before I go." He tugged at his shirt, revealing golden dots of some kind of oil on his light blue shirt. A smear of bike-shop goo on his left cheek could have been anything from mud to motor fluids.

"I'll leave you to it," Molly said, and turned to go, only to glance back. "I put fresh towels in your bathroom and there's plenty of hot water. I'll be praying *Gott's* will for your life."

His hand on the doorknob, Isaac said, "*Danke*, Molly. I need those prayers."

"You can pray, too, you know. Where two or more are praying, He's in the midst of them."

Isaac's head dropped. "Sometimes I think *Gott* doesn't listen to my prayers anymore."

Molly paused. Isaac stood inches from her, prepared to shut his bedroom door behind her. She really didn't know anything about his life, his family, what he believed, but she did know he was hardworking and kind. Since showing up at their door, the road-weary expression he wore on his face convinced her there were things undone in his spiritual life. Threads that had unraveled, leaving him feeling alone and lost. She knew what that loneliness felt like.

When her sister, Greta, had died suddenly in childbirth, it had taken Molly a long time to trust God again, to believe He knew what was best for her life. Maybe Isaac was going through loss, too. She smiled her encouragement. "You'll see. Just pray for *Gott*'s will and wait for the good to happen."

Chapter Nine

There was no hesitation in Isaac's steps. He strolled up to Mose's furniture store as if he didn't have a care in the world. He wanted to exude confidence. His pain level down, his limp was less noticeable and not as apt to hold him back.

He remembered Molly's words about prayer and whispered, *Gott, let this meeting go well. Give me the right words. Have Your will in my life.*

He opened the main door. A bell announced his arrival. He stepped into the furniture showroom and wiped his feet on the rough, fibrous floor mat underfoot. The barnlike building, full of beautiful handmade furniture, amazed him. There was no lack of stock here. Mose Fischer was obviously an intelligent and talented man with a thriving business.

A man dressed Amish, but one Isaac didn't recognize, waved from the back of the store. "*Willkumm*, I'll be right with you." Tall, well-built and obviously energetic, his movements were quick and fluid as he finished wrapping the desk next to him, coating it in plastic wrap to protect the finish for shipping.

"How are you this fine morning?" The man approached. He extended his hand and grasped Isaac's in a powerful handshake that told Isaac the man had lifted heavy furniture for years.

One of the man's fingers flicked his name badge. "Name's Fredrik, but people 'round here often call me Fred." He grinned, keeping the conversation friendly.

"*Gut* to meet you, Fred." Isaac put his hand behind his back and flexed blood back into his fingers. He had to work on his upper body strength, not just his legs. Since the wreck he'd lost considerable weight and muscle tone. Too much time lying in a hospital bed.

"What is it you're looking for? A bed, or perhaps a table for your new *haus*?" The man moved from side to side, flicking his dust rag from his pocket and polishing the tables nearby as he spoke.

Isaac liked the man's work ethic. He'd need this kind of employee one day if he could ever get the business off the ground and start making enough profit to hire someone ambitious. "No, I'm not a customer today. I was hoping to talk to Mose Fischer for a moment if he's in."

"*Ach*, and me running my mouth about furniture." The man grinned from ear to ear, as only the young and eager did. He pointed to a room just off to the side of the building. "That would be his office. Just give a knock. He'll call you in if he's not on the phone with business. It's good to meet you, Herr…"

"Graber, Isaac Graber." He suffered through another crushing handshake.

"*Gut* to meet you, Herr Graber. You come see us before your wedding day. We can fill your home with beautiful furniture."

"I'm not getting married anytime soon." Isaac thought of his pretend courting with Molly, but they had no future together. Their ruse meant absolutely nothing.

Turning to head back to his work, Fredrik murmured, "Oh, you will be. And soon. *Ya*, all the signs are there."

"Signs?" Isaac asked the man, staring at his broad back.

The man stopped and turned toward Isaac.

"*Ya*, signs. You're young and single. That's all it takes to get tangled up with one of the smart Amish women here in Pinecraft. Lots are looking for husbands." He laughed like he knew all the secrets of the world and headed to the back of the store, whistling the same song Molly had been singing that morning.

The hair on his arms stood up as he walked across the shiny tile floor to Mose's office. He knocked, glancing back at Mose's busy employee while he waited.

Mose Fischer opened the door, the man's blond hair a messy nest of curls covered in sawdust. "Good to see you again, Isaac. Hope the shop's doing well."

The men shook hands and Isaac flinched.

"I see you've meet Fredrik," Mose commented. "He has quite a handshake, doesn't he?"

Isaac laughed, trying to hide his embarrassment. "I thought he'd squeeze my hand off. I'd better start lifting weights before I come back to buy furniture."

Mose motioned for Isaac to sit in a comfortable-looking chair. He moved behind an old, scratched desk and dropped into a squeaky computer chair. "I'd never considered myself a weakling until I hired Fredrik a couple of years ago. He had me pumping iron just to endure his morning greetings," Mose added with a smile. "So what can I do for you? A new desk and computer chair for your office?" Bright blue eyes gazed at him expectantly.

Isaac breathed deeply. "I came to talk to you about the church. Well, not exactly the church, but the chance of a church loan. I could pay it back in say…five years, give or take a year."

"A loan for business or personal?" Mose pulled at his long beard, his forehead creased.

"Business."

"How much do you need?"

Isaac slumped in his chair. He had no idea how much money he needed. He hadn't thought that far ahead, convinced he'd be laughed out of the man's office as soon as he opened his mouth about borrowing church money.

He straightened, looked Mose in the eyes and sputtered. "I…well, I was thinking of a couple new golf carts and several really nice new bikes to sell, not rent. Having stock would help pick up profits and maybe fill the shelves with parts. *Ya*, parts, lots of them because I'm sick of turning away customers because I don't have what they need." Isaac stopped talking because Mose was smiling broadly, as if he was ready to burst into laughter, just as Isaac feared.

"You remind me of myself all those years ago," Mose said. "I was young and fresh as a corn cob that had fallen off the back of my *daed*'s truck. I had no idea what I'd need to get this furniture business off the ground, but it was my heart's desire and I was willing to do whatever it took. Even fight for it if I had to, and I did. My *daed* wanted me to be a farmer, like him. He made my life miserable for years. I went to *Gott* with my problem and He set the path, just like He set yours when you came in here today, ready to do battle for your dream."

Isaac swallowed a lump in his throat. Mose had seen his vision, felt his earnest desire to make his business grow. *Danke, Gott.* "I was afraid you'd laugh at me."

"Laugh? *Nee*, not laugh. But I will speak as your representative to my father, Otto Fischer. He's the community bishop and calls the financial committee together for requests such as this. I usually head those committees, so rest easy. You'll get a fair hearing. You should know our answer in a few days, a week at most. Hold on to your faith. If this is *Gott*'s will, all will go well. And relax. You look wound tighter than a kettledrum."

Isaac considered telling Mose about his past, but shame held him back. "*Danke*, Mose.

You've been so helpful. I can't thank you enough for—"

Mose cut him off. "There's no need for thanks, Isaac. Just remember. The community of Pinecraft is here for you. You seem to have made a good impression on Molly, and I trust her judgment."

Isaac's gaze veered away. "Molly's a kind woman, full of promise. Someday she'll make a wonderful, spirited wife."

"That she will, but I don't want her hurt by anyone."

Isaac laughed a little. Mose didn't have to worry about him. He had no interest in falling in love with anyone, especially Molly. "She's a good friend. You don't have to worry about me. I'm no threat to Molly's happiness. For now, my mind is set on work, and nothing more."

"But hearts grow close at the least expected time. I know from experience. Don't pull Molly into your life if you have no real intentions toward her. Let her get on with her search to find someone she can love if you feel so strongly about using your time and energy to build your business. All I had to offer my Sarah was a promise of a future. Little more than hard work and my rambunctious *kinner* to care for. She jumped at the chance. Molly might, too, if you show the least bit of interest."

Isaac rose and extended his sore hand. "*Danke*, Mose for your help with the loan… and the good advice. *Gott* has a plan for my life, and I don't want to be out of His will ever again."

The sun woke Molly an hour early the next morning. In a hurry to get out the door, she dressed quickly and rushed to eat a bowl of cereal, only to get waylaid by her mother at the kitchen table and caught up in an argument.

"I don't want to talk about Samuel again. You know I don't love him, *Mamm*." She spoke over her empty cereal bowl. "He's not my type and I'm…" Her voice trailed off, weary of the fight. She was tired of being treated like a child because she wasn't married. She'd said all this before, but each chapter and verse of her argument was being ignored.

"You have little option, Molly. This foolishness about Isaac has to stop. He's not the man for you. He's as poor as a church mouse and has no future to offer you," Ulla said from across the table.

Molly rose and faced her mother. "I don't want to marry without love, and I don't love

Samuel." Her mother's expression reflected grim determination. She shoved her coffee cup into the hot water glistening with suds, silently praying her mother would be reasonable just this once.

Dressed in a freshly ironed dress of navy blue, her apron heavily starched, Ulla wiped her mouth on a linen napkin and then pushed away from the breakfast table. She slammed her plate against the kitchen counter. "I said forget about Isaac. After church this Sunday, I want you to tell Samuel that you *do* love him. Explain that you were just testing the waters, do you hear?" She moved away, rammed her chair back under the table and headed for the door, her steps quick and angry. "You have to marry the man. We need his money to keep the boarding *haus* open. Too many of our seasonal renters have passed on to be with the Lord. New hotels are opening all around us. Each winter we are left with the crumbs; the leftovers no one else wants to rent to. If we are to survive—"

"You mean if *you* are to survive, *Mamm*. Money was never an issue when *Daed* was alive and running this home. You insist on buying what we don't need, spending money on things you want. Your knickknacks and whatnots clutter this house." Molly lifted a wooden chicken off the counter and held it up for her mother to see. "I won't sacrifice my life to pay for your expensive trinkets. If Samuel is such a good catch, you marry him. I'm not—"

Ulla walked over to Molly and grabbed her arm with steely fingers. Anger pressed her mother's features into a harsh scowl. "I have sacrificed all my life for you. It is time you sacrificed for me."

Molly jerked out of her mother's grasp and stood her ground. "*Nee*, not anymore. I have done all I am going to do. A loveless marriage is where I draw the line."

Her eyes narrow slits, Ulla leaned close and poked Molly on the chest. "You are Amish and unmarried. You will do as you are told. I will not allow this behavior to go on in *mein haus*. When you see Samuel, make it clear you are prepared to court and marry."

Turning on her heel, her *mamm* slammed out of the house, leaving Molly slumped against the kitchen counter.

The time had come for drastic changes. She had to take a stand or be railroaded into something she didn't want. Her mother had gone too far.

She looked around the room. She'd grown up

in this house. Most of her happy moments with Greta were experienced here. They'd laughed together in this kitchen as *kinner*. And cried together, as well. They'd shared the big double bed until the day her sister married Mose Fischer. Her sister's book of poems were hidden in Molly's clothes drawer, along with the *kapp* Greta had worn the day she'd died. There were no pictures of her to look at and remember. Just memories from the past.

Molly didn't wait for her thoughts to clear. She wasn't going to stay in this *haus* a moment longer. She'd bring her suitcases to work with her, work her shift and later go to Mose and Sarah's for wisdom.

They lived in Pinecraft, where church rules were often bent and twisted. She saw no reason why she shouldn't become more independent. She was twenty-one now, after all. An adult. She didn't have to live under her *mamm*'s thumb or be forced into a loveless marriage.

Sarah had gone through a lot back in Lancaster. She was a *gut* person to ask for wisdom, and Mose would keep her in line, help her not break Ordnung rules. She didn't want trouble with her church, or the Bishop. She loved Otto Fischer like a father and respected his position in the community.

Packed and ready to leave, Molly walked through the house, touching the chair her father had always sat in. His place at the table was still held in reserve out of respect. His death had come as a powerful blow to Molly and Greta. She'd tried hard to accept *Gott*'s will for her life but secretly resented *Gott* for taking her father so soon, and then Greta.

Walking into the great room for one last time, she grabbed a sheet of writing paper from the desk and wrote with heavy strokes of the pen.

Mamm,
I need to get away and think. Please don't
look for me.
Molly

She pushed her note away from the edge of the table and walked out the front door, her small zippered suitcases beating against her thighs as she hurried to the driveway.

With her legs pumping fast, she rode her bike to the café, parked in the back and pulled her bags from the basket. She rushed in through the employees' door, her two small suitcases in hand, pretending everything was fine. She felt gutted inside, her stomach heaving, but she had customers to feed, hard work to do when her shift began in a half hour. Work would keep her mind off things best not thought about. Like her *mamm*'s reaction to her moving out. She put on her apron, looked through the windows toward Isaac's shop and saw a Closed sign hanging on the door handle.

She turned and headed to the kitchen.

The grill spit and sputtered hamburger fat all over the thick cotton apron stretched across Willa Mae's generous figure. The older woman turned toward Molly, her spatula flipping meat patties with precision. She'd had years of practice. "Hey, you look like someone ran over your favorite cat. What's up, Sugar?"

"*Ach*, you don't want to know." All morning she'd been able to think of nothing but Isaac and her mother, but now that Willa Mae was standing in front of her, she questioned her decision. Maybe she'd acted too rashly when she'd packed her bags. Was moving out a good idea? Mose would probably advise her she should have waited and prayed for *Gott*'s direction, but she'd had enough of her *mamm*'s demands. She would not marry Samuel without love.

Willa Mae flipped a rare burger on the toasted bottom bun, slathered it with mayonnaise and then slapped on a tomato slice, lettuce leaves and two rings of red onion on the mustard-covered top bun. "Sure, I wanna know. Spill it. Tell your mean ole boss what's on your mind." She sandwiched the two halves together and leaned on the mountain of food, squeezing it down to a reasonable height before she slid it on a plate already lined with potato chips.

How could she tell her what was going on without sounding like a spoiled child? "It's my *mamm*."

"Ulla again? What did she do this time? Make you eat your greens?" Willa Mae put the plate through the food window and bellowed like a pig farmer, "Food's up." She jerked down the next slip of paper from the roundabout and read the food order, her lips moving. "I know she treats you like a nine-year-old and shows you no respect. So what's new?"

Molly picked up a pickle slice and popped it in her mouth. The sour flavor puckered her lips and made her cheeks hurt. "She's really crossed the line this time."

"You said that the last four times you came into this kitchen grumbling. You're gonna have to come up with something fresh if you're gonna keep my interest piqued." Her deep, throaty laugh, the result of too many packs of cigarettes twenty years ago, filled the small kitchen. She coughed and wheezed into the sleeve of her chef's uniform and then went back to work at the grill.

"She told Samuel he could court me and she didn't even ask how I felt about him. She had no right. I was so embarrassed, and now she says I have to marry him, like it or not."

Willa Mae broke an egg with one hand and then broke another. They sizzled on the hot grill. Two strips of bacon joined the eggs and instantly shriveled. "Isn't he that rich Amish kid, the big-time farmer from Ohio?" Two slices of light wheat toast popped up, perfectly brown and ready for a brush of melted butter.

"*Ya*, his family's got money, but—"

Willa Mae cut Molly off. "Look, child. He's got money. Your mama likes spending money. Makes perfect sense to me. If I was young enough, I'd marry him myself. Anything to get away from this hot stove." The piping hot plate of food was shoved through the food window, followed by two tiny containers overflowing with pickles. "Food's up."

Molly caught Willa Mae's gaze and saw confusion in her honey-brown eyes. "I'm a twenty-one-year-old spinster. I live with my domineering mother, work two jobs. I've never courted seriously, and I'm supposed to marry Samuel for his money. Does that help you understand?" Tears welled up in her eyes, making everything go blurry around her.

Willa Mae moved in closer, her arm slipping around Molly's trembling shoulders. "Oh, don't be starting no tears up in here. I'm sorry you're sad, honey. I really am. I thought this was just one of your usual rants. I didn't know you were really upset, or I wouldn't have teased you."

Molly cried like a child all over her boss's shoulder. "I've been pretending to court Isaac, but I think he may have a girlfriend back home."

"Wait up a minute. Who has a girlfriend? I thought we were talking about your mama forcing Samuel on you. Keep it simple for me, honey. I'm old as dirt and I can't keep up with your rambling."

Molly's bottom lip trembled. She sniffed, taking the dish towel her boss thrust at her. It smelled of bacon grease and tomatoes. She wiped her eyes, but the tears kept flowing. "This man I've been seeing, Isaac… I think he might have a girlfriend. He got a letter from somebody named Rose, and we're supposed to be courting, or pretending to be courting. If she comes here for a visit and is truly his girlfriend, how will we keep up our ruse?" Molly groaned. "Oh, I don't know. I'm just so emotional lately."

Willa Mae nodded, her dark ringlets, covered by a hairnet, dancing on her head. "Let me see if I've got this right." She splayed out her fingers and started counting off offenses. "Your mom upset you by trying to sell you to the highest bidder?"

Molly nodded. *"Ya."*

"And you and some guy named Isaac are mixed up in some kind of ruse, and now his girlfriend might come to Pinecraft and spoil all your plans?" Willa Mae's brow arched. "How am I doing so far?"

Molly pulled on her prayer *kapp* ribbons. "You forgot the part where I packed my bags and moved out and have no place to live."

"Oh, girl. You've gone and done it this time. Your mama's gonna run wild through the streets looking for you by this time tomorrow, and this café is the first place she's likely to come. What do you want me to tell her?" Willa Mae frowned as she flicked another order off the roundabout, threw a small steak on the grill and then dunked a basket of fries into hot, bubbling oil.

Molly dropped into the chair near the back window and put her head in her hands. "I don't know. I haven't thought any of this through. I've made a real mess of my life, and no one's to blame but myself."

Molly wanted to scream in frustration. What had she gotten herself into?

Chapter Ten

Damp and miserable, Molly dodged rain puddles as she hurried through the streets of Pinecraft, the sky darkening with the promise of more rain. Mose and Sarah's home was only a couple of blocks away from the café, but Molly was tired from a long day at work. The short distance felt like miles.

The Lapps' baby had taken hours to deliver, hours with nothing to do but wait, think and panic. In her mind her problems had become insurmountable, more than she could deal with without good counsel. She'd called Mose in desperation, asked if she could come to the house as soon as she was free. Now she wished she hadn't. Talking would just add to her stress. But Mose might have a solution, something she could do that didn't include tucking her tail between her legs and going back home.

Someone had left the porch light on, a beacon of hope in the shimmery drizzle soaking her hair and dress. She ran up to the door, knocked and heard the high-pitched squeal of children. Sarah opened the door, her smile welcoming, a circle of blond-haired children clustered around her skirt.

"Come in, Molly," she said, speaking over small voices demanding they get to their aunt first. "Beatrice, take your aunt's bag and then run and get a towel from the bathroom. She looks wet and tired."

"Why do I have to get it? You never ask Mercy to do anything." Beatrice's fake tears gathered in her eyes.

"Go," Sarah insisted. "You don't want your aunt Molly to think you're not my biggest helper, do you?"

"Nee," the little girl groaned, her small bare feet slapping against the polished tile floor as she ran toward the back of the house.

Mercy climbed like a monkey, her small arms wrapping tightly around Molly's neck. She offered up a huge, toothy grin. "I free now," she said, and held up four tiny fingers.

Molly pretended to bite at her fingers. The little girl giggled and snuggled her head into Molly's neck.

Mose walked into the room and relieved Molly of her wiggling bundle. "Let's give your aunt a drink and a slice of your mom's strudel before you overwhelm her with hugs and kisses." He smiled at Molly. "You look like you've had a difficult day."

Molly patted her blond-haired nephew's head. Levi had grown since she'd last seen him. He was tall for almost two and strikingly beautiful for a boy. He grinned up at her, his arms clamped on to her leg like a vise. She returned his smile and told Mose, "*Ya*, I did. Just as I was leaving my shift I got the call. My patient wasn't due for another week, but babies decide when it's time to come, convenient or not. The mom's fine and her son's a gorgeous *bobbel*. I'm sure she'll be showing him off at church next week."

Sarah rubbed her own protruding stomach, smiling. "Why don't you come in, instead of standing at the door?" She took Molly's arm, and they strolled toward the kitchen. "Let me grab you some strudel, hot from the oven. We can sit and talk."

Beatrice ran in, a white hand towel clutched to her chest. "Here, Molly."

"Thank you, *liebling*. You're such a good girl." Molly took the towel and patted her face and neck dry before bending to give the child a tender kiss on the cheek. Beatrice glowed, her love for her aunt reflected in her deep blue eyes. "I went to visit *Grossmammi* today. She said—"

"We don't want to hear what Ulla said, Beatrice. She should not speak of adult things around you. It would be best if you learn not to repeat what she tells you," Mose instructed. "Find your little sister and brother and take them into the playroom, and mind that you are kind to them. No angry words. Do you hear?" His hand propelled the sulking child toward the back of the house. "Sometimes I wish… Never mind what I wish. Let's forget about Beatrice being so like Ulla and eat our strudel." A growing smile wiped the frown from his face.

The kitchen was warm and inviting, the fragrance of freshly baked pastry hanging heavy in the air. Molly eased herself into a chair and forced a smile. "Thank you for allowing me to come."

Sarah, busy plating slices of hot pastry, returned Molly's smile. "You are always welcome here. You know that."

A tear trailed down Molly's cheek, then another.

"Oh, what's wrong?" Sarah said, and hurried over, putting her arms around Molly's shoulders.

"I've made such a mess of things," Molly groaned.

Mose pulled out a chair and sat, a look of concern creasing his face. "What's happened?" He pressed a napkin into her hand.

Molly dried her eyes, her chin wobbling, new tears threatening. "I moved out."

Sarah spoke to Mose under her breath. "I suspected this would happen."

Dabbing at her eyes, Molly released a deep sigh. "It's Samuel Bawell."

"Ah…I'd wondered." Mose rubbed at his beard. "For a while there's been talk that a courtship has begun between the two of you."

"I know, but it's not true. I don't love him, or his money." She lifted her head and looked Mose in the eyes. "I promise you I didn't lead him on. It's *Mamm*. She keeps pushing me, insisting I encourage Samuel's attention. Telling him to pursue me. I'm not interested in courting and marriage right now. Well, not with Samuel anyway." She thought of Isaac, his dark hair shining in the sun across the picnic table, just before he told her he wasn't interested in courting her. She took in a shuddering breath.

Patting Molly's hand, Sarah asked, "And you've told Ulla this, made yourself clear?"

"*Ya*, I've done everything but stand on my head and shout my words at her. She just won't listen. All she speaks of is the man's connections, his big farm. The money he has."

"Where are you staying?" Sarah asked, squeezing Molly's hand.

"I don't know yet," Molly said in a raspy voice laden with tears.

"Moving out wasn't the best course to take, Molly," Mose said, his tone that of a big brother. "It's not proper for a young woman to live alone. This world is a dangerous place. Especially for a young, innocent girl like you. You need to think hard about this. Your mother could have you banned from the church, and my father's hands would be tied. Otto will not break Ordnung rules for anyone, not even you, *liebling*."

Molly blinked. "*Mamm*'s already threatened to talk to your *daed*, but I'm not going back." Molly's eyes grew bright with determination. "I won't!"

* * *

A restless night of tossing and turning at Mose and Sarah's *haus* brought no relief to Molly's troubled mind. She wiped the sweat off her brow with a napkin and washed her hands for the millionth time. The café had been busy all day, and a half hour past closing time the stragglers were still asking for another cup of coffee or piece of pie.

She wanted to tell everyone to go home, walk out the door, but she put on her happy face and kept cleaning tables and booths, running for food when Willa Mae called out.

"How many customers we got now?"

Molly grabbed a hot plate of fries and dropped an empty ketchup bottle into the trash. "Two couples and a strange little man who's having a great time talking to himself."

"He's not dangerous, is he?" Willa Mae scraped at the cooling grill, removing a day's layer of fat and bits of egg white.

"*Nee*, not dangerous. He seems harmless enough." Molly wiped down the food window while she talked, glancing over her shoulder every few seconds to keep an eye on the front of the café.

"I called my landlady a minute ago. She's

got a place near me, but it's an efficiency in her motel, 'bout the size of a closet."

Molly could feel her face morphing from happy smile to worried frown. "Exactly how big is it?"

"She said maybe fourteen by fourteen feet, but it's furnished and even has kitchen supplies." Willa Mae's smile was warm and bright, her teeth flashing white in the fluorescent lighting as if she'd just told Molly she'd just won the lottery. "She said you can rent it for as long as you need to. Two days, a month. It doesn't matter to her, and it's better than what you've got now. Nothing."

The ugly truth hit Molly. Willa Mae was right. A small room was better than a park bench, and that was her plan B. "You think the room comes with sheets, too?"

"What you want for two hundred dollars a week? A swimming pool and spa?" Willa Mae pulled off her apron and reached for her walking shoes. "We closing this place down in five minutes, girl. Don't let nobody in and don't take no more orders. The grill's clean and the coffeepots washed. No fill-ups."

Molly walked to the front and locked the main door, trying to imagine a living room, bedroom and kitchen in one room. She gave up. It couldn't be done. Molly's head began to thump. Her feet already hurt, and she was tired of smelling French fries and fried beef patties. All she wanted was a hot shower and some sleep.

She made her way to the kitchen and watched as her boss washed her arms up to her elbows. "If I take the place, can I move in tonight?" She didn't know what she'd do if the answer was no. Willa Mae had offered her a bed, but she had three half-grown kids and a grumpy husband. Her boss was being the kindhearted woman Pinecraft knew her to be, but Molly didn't want to put her out, even for a night, and she'd bothered Sarah and Mose enough. Sarah was pregnant. She didn't need the extra work.

"I'll ring her and see what she says. She's probably still up. She watches lots of TV, like us old folk do. You'll probably be able to hear it in your apartment. She's that close."

Molly grimaced as she reached up to straighten her *kapp*.

"We all got to learn to be grateful for what we get in life, girl." Willa Mae continued, "God don't like no whiny kid crying to Him 'bout hardship."

Molly smiled her apology. She was ashamed of her own childishness. "Thank you for calling your friend about the apartment. I'm sorry. I was being silly. I'm just scared."

She could see her own reflection in Willa Mae's dark eyes.

"None of us is perfect, child." Her smile grew. "She might give you a discount. She likes to rent to you Amish folk. Says you pay on time and never run out on her."

"I know you're right about the apartment. I just had dreams." Molly brushed down her white apron, ashamed of herself.

Willa Mae put her arm across Molly's shoulders and squeezed. "We all have dreams. I wanted to be a famous movie star and make lots of money, but God said, 'You be the best cook you can be.' I didn't go to Hollywood, but I did get this place and my kids. That's enough. Sometimes enough has to be enough, Molly." She laughed, her belly jiggling. "You're young, but smart. One day you gonna meet some nice Amish man like that Isaac fella and get married. Children become your dream and a clean house your job. You'll see if I'm not right."

Molly thought of Isaac and a tiny boy with dark hair like his *daed*. She smiled, but then remembered she and Isaac were just pretending to court. He wouldn't be her children's father, but *Gott* would send someone someday, and he'd be a perfect match for her when she was ready. She believed that with all her heart.

Asked to come along as moral support an hour later, Isaac held the door as Molly and Lalalu, the motel manager, stepped into the apartment. The word *tiny* instantly came to Molly's mind. She looked at Isaac, and he shrugged, silently telling her he had no opinion.

The room looked clean and didn't smell.

Molly put on a brave face and handed over two crisp hundred-dollar bills. Lalalu looked both bills over carefully and then handed her a single key. Molly smiled her appreciation, grateful to have a place to lay her head for the next week.

Short, bony and her hair wild as if a tornado had styled it, Lalalu grinned and exposed gaps in her upper teeth. "Willa Mae said you're dependable and a hard worker. That's good enough for me." A remarkable underbite left the woman's jaw jutting like a bulldog's. The colorful caftan she wore dragged on the floor as she pointed out a miniature bathroom off the back of the room.

Molly stuck her head through the open door. Most of the bathroom's floor space was taken up by a walk-in shower with a plastic flamingo shower curtain that spilled out against a bowl-sized sink. The toilet was shoved into a corner of the room and low to the ground. The white fixtures sparkled clean and bright under a bare light bulb hanging from the ceiling.

Isaac stuck his head in the confining space and rubbed his clean-shaven jaw. "Big enough for one," he remarked, and backed out into the living quarters.

"I won't charge you a deposit, honey. I know you'll be straight up with me. My Amish tenants are always tidy and quiet and pay on time."

"*Danke*, I promise you I won't be a bother." Molly followed as her new landlady walked to the side of the bedroom.

"This here's your kitchen area."

Molly glanced at the wall across from the bathroom door. A short butcher-block counter had a mini-sink and backsplash, as well as two regular-sized electric burners. Wooden shelves lined with apple-trimmed paper held a plate, glass, two cups and a stack of saucepans. Molly glanced around, looking for a table to eat at and realized there was none. Not even a small one.

"I don't supply TVs, but you can bring one in if you want."

Molly blinked at her and blinked again. She'd read *Alice in Wonderland* as a child and felt just like Alice must have felt falling down the rabbit hole.

"I don't watch television." She straightened her *kapp* and tugged both ribbons to pull it down tighter on her head.

Isaac put his hand on the small of her back and then stepped aside as Molly moved to the bed. "Do you supply sheets, or will I need my own?" The bed looked made up, but perhaps there was just a bedspread on it for show.

Lalalu threw back the flowered spread and exposed white sheets neatly tucked in the foot of the bed. "We got you covered, Molly. I washed those sheets this afternoon and line dried them the way you Amish like." She grinned as she glided back toward the apartment door. "I probably don't need to tell you, but I'm gonna do it anyway." Her bony finger pointed toward Molly. "You're my renter. Not him." She frowned at Isaac, her forehead crinkling into a road map of lines. "There's to be no overnight guests." Her eyes cut to Molly and then back to Isaac. "No loud music and no lounging in the yard in a bathing suit," she advised in a carefree way.

"*Ya*, sure. That sounds fine. I'll obey the rules."

"I know you will," the older woman said,

then glanced Isaac's way again. "But what about you?"

Molly cringed as Isaac looked up, flushed red and then nodded. "*Ya*. That all sounds fine to me."

"Good. Now you let me know if you need anything, Molly," Lalalu murmured, then went out the door and shut it softly behind her.

The room was silent.

Molly could hear Isaac breathing.

She latched the dead bolt and wiggled the doorknob, making sure it locked and smiled at him nervously. "The deed is done."

"*Ya*," he said, watching her. "No going back now." His eyes darkened. Was he concerned for her? Tonight would be the first time in her life she was completely alone.

She wandered around the room with Isaac trailing behind her at an easy pace. She checked out the apartment-sized refrigerator under the kitchen cabinet. The freezer compartment held an empty tray for ice, which left little room for anything else. The inside of the fridge was clean and smelled fresh.

She sniffed the new white dish towel hanging on a nail and smiled, the feeling of ownership finally sinking in. She had her own place, somewhere to come to after long days at the café.

"I'd better go before Lalalu comes back and kicks me out," Isaac said, edging for the door.

"*Danke* for coming with me tonight."

"You have to know I'm not sure about all this, Molly." Isaac took another step toward the door.

"*Ya*, well. Mose thinks I'm making a mistake, too, but I had to take a stand."

His hand on the doorknob, Isaac cleared his throat. "Make sure you lock this latch behind me."

"I will."

"Call me if you have any problems or…well, you know. Get scared or something."

"I'm not a *kinner*, Isaac. I should be fine." She fingered the key to her newfound freedom and slipped it into her apron pocket.

"*Ya*, I'll see you tomorrow."

She tugged at her prayer *kapp* ribbons. "Tomorrow."

The door shut behind him, and Molly locked the dead bolt. She saw the door handle wiggle. Isaac had checked to make sure she'd remembered that lock, too.

Alone at last she dropped to the edge of the bed and then jumped to her feet as the sound of a blaring television invaded the silence of the tiny room. *Lalalu must be watching television.*

She unpacked, putting her starched and ironed *kapps* and what few things she owned on a shelf in the makeshift closet by the bed. She hung her church dress, two aprons and several everyday work dresses side by side and swished the tablecloth, hung from a string and two nails, closed.

Tired beyond words, she crawled into the surprisingly comfortable bed and lay on her back, listening to the muffled voices and Lalalu's laughter. She drifted off to sleep, her last conscious thought a prayer for Isaac. *Gott, keep him safe and don't let* Mamm *kick him out of the house before he finds a new place to stay.*

Chapter Eleven

Not wanting a confrontation with Ulla before he found a permanent place to live, Isaac showered, dressed and slipped out of his rental room before seeing the older woman.

He opened the bike shop and greeted two waiting customers. Molly's situation hovered at the back of his mind as he rented his last two big-seated bikes to two round-faced Amish women with heart-shaped *kapps* signifying connections to an Old Order community up north. Their crisp money would look nice in the drawer.

His cell phone rang, and he answered the call with a good-humored smile in his voice, even though he still wasn't used to the Pinecraft custom of using a phone for his business needs. "The Bike Pit, Isaac speaking." He dropped into his computer chair, pride of ownership giving him a sense of peace as he waited for his caller to speak.

"Otto Fischer here. You got a minute to meet at the café?"

Isaac's smile vanished. This meeting had to be about the church loan. He rubbed his aching leg and propped it on a box of bike tubes. "*Ya*, I do have time. I can see you in five minutes, if that works for you."

"*Ya*, I got all day and nothing to do. I'll see you soon."

What if he didn't get the loan? Would a bank consider him a good risk? He doubted it. He had no credit history, no experience as a salesman or repairman. He shoved the cell phone in his pants pocket. *I need Gott's will for my life more than ever.*

His empty stomach growled, reminding him he hadn't eaten since supper, and that had been a pack of peanut butter crackers. Maybe he'd eat a plate of pumpkin pancakes while he waited for the bishop. He took several fives out of the drawer, wrote the money draw in the book and locked up the shop.

Inside the busy café, an empty booth offered him a chance to sit down. Hurrying over, Isaac crossed paths with several customers. He slid across the booth's red leather seat before anyone else could snatch up the spot, and stretched out his aching leg. He didn't bother checking the menu. He already knew what he wanted. A stack of steaming pancakes with lots of syrup and a couple of sausages, but he had to wait for Otto. The fragrant aroma of the hot café was killing him.

"Hello." Molly came up behind Isaac and greeted him with a shy smile.

"You slept well last night?" he asked, eyeing the dark circles under Molly's eyes.

"*Nee*, I didn't get much sleep. You?"

"Like you, I tossed and turned. I'm meeting with Bishop Fischer today, and it's important."

Molly wiped down the table and placed a fresh cup of coffee in front of him. "Has *Mamm* said anything to you?" She leaned in close, pretending to wipe down the saltshaker. "She could make your life difficult."

"I left early and avoided her, but that can't go on forever, Molly. We need to talk, get our stories straight."

"*Ya*, I don't like what all this deception is doing to you. Perhaps my plan was a mistake. Maybe I just need to stand up to her and Samuel, speak more firmly."

Isaac took a sip of the black coffee she poured. "Standing up to him hasn't worked so far."

Molly's shoulders drooped. "*Nee*, he is a stubborn man, used to getting his way, but I can be stubborn, too, when pushed into a corner."

"We need to talk tomorrow and work out what's to be done."

Isaac glanced up and saw Otto Fischer walk into the café. The old man glanced around, then hurried over. "*Guder mariye*, Molly. And you are well today?" He sat and tossed his hat on the table.

"*Ya*, I'm *gut*. And you?" Molly asked.

Isaac watched their exchange of words and tried to get a feel of the man's mood, but Otto Fischer gave no secrets away, his expression calm, as always. He was a quiet man, one who spoke only when he had something to say.

"*Gott* is good, and I have no complaints worthy of hearing." The old man grinned.

"I'll send your waitress over quick as I can." Molly poured Otto a steaming cup of coffee. "You two enjoy your breakfast," she said, and hurried back to the kitchen.

Otto faced Isaac "Have you ordered yet?"

"*Nee*, I waited for you."

"Let's get our food ordered and then we talk." He motioned for the blonde-haired waitress at the back of the café and tossed aside the menu as she walked their way. "*Hallich geburtsdaag*, Heidi. Your special day is *gut*, *ya*?"

"*Danke*, Grossdaddi! But I had to work on my birthday. One of the girls called in sick. I couldn't tell Willa Mae no, but later there is a party in my honor. You and *Grossmammi* will come?"

"I wouldn't miss the chance to call you an old maid now that you've turned eighteen."

"Grossdaddi, you are terrible." Laughing, the blonde-haired, blue-eyed teen gave her grandfather a fleeting kiss on the cheek.

"So your *grossmammi* keeps telling me." His expression glowed with love for the blonde-haired girl. "She's made a special treat for you, like when you were a *kinner* and she spoiled you with too much attention. You'll be surprised."

"Is it strudel, with lots of apples?" The girl's smile brightened.

"Time will tell all things, *liebling*. Patience is a gift from *Gott*."

Heidi gave her grandfather a hug, and turned his coffee cup over. "Coffee?"

"*Ya*, *kaffi* sounds *gut* and a stack of Willa Mae's special peanut butter pancakes for your favorite *grossdaddi*."

Still grinning as she poured from a steaming carafe of coffee, Heidi filled his cup, her gaze turning to Isaac. She poured coffee into his waiting cup when he nodded. "And you, sir. Pancakes, too?"

Isaac grinned. "Pumpkin pancakes for me, with sausage, *bitte*, and ask for my syrup to be warmed."

"*Ya*, I will." She hurried off, her skirt swirling.

"I didn't know you had grown grandchildren, Bishop."

"Heidi is *mei* oldest son Ruben's child. She is a good girl, and we are proud of her, but we did not gather here to speak of my family. It is the loan you are interested in talking about."

Isaac took a sip of coffee and nodded. "It is. I wouldn't ask for help if I had another choice. It's time to swallow my pride."

"Pride is a sin, Isaac. At your age you should already know this. We strive to be like *Gott* and accept His guidance and instruction. You play an important part of our community now. We often help new businesses flourish." He smiled at Isaac. "I have talked with the elders, and I think we've found a plan that will work well for all of us."

Heidi carried over two white plates topped with stacks of perfectly browned pancakes, breakfast sausages and two jugs of warm syrup. "This should keep you two going for a while." She topped up their coffees and smiled. "Just wave if you need anything."

There was silence at the table as both men prayed silently and then dug in to their food. Isaac laid down his fork when his belly was full and watched Otto Fischer take his last bite of pancake. "This plan you speak of. How will it work to both our advantages?"

"The church will become partners with you for a time. We will buy a share of your business, and you can use the cash to add stock, increase your business, whatever you need. If you work hard, you'll make a go of the bike shop. We will continue to back you financially until you are steady on your feet, and in the black for a time. Then you can buy us out, and we will help another new business."

"*Ya*, this plan is a good one," Isaac said and watched as his bishop nodded his agreement.

"The elders would be happier if you were a married *mann* with a family, or at least courting. Is there a girl?"

Molly walked out of the kitchen, her blue dress covered in a work apron splattered with food. Sunlight danced off her dark hair as she walked past the café window. She glanced to-

ward their booth and her gaze locked with
Isaac's for seconds. She hurried back into the
kitchen, but her sudden shy smile told him she
was glad to have seen him.

"There's one I'm considering, but I'm not
sure the time will ever be right."

The next morning loud conversation woke
Molly with a start. She shoved her covers off
her shoulders and then froze, listening. The
forceful voice had the unmistakable high-
pitched superiority her mother used when trying to make her point.

"Mamm," she whispered, falling back among
her pillows and pulling the covers over her
head. She knew she'd find her. People talked
in Pinecraft, but she had hoped for more than
a day to prepare for the onslaught.

Just as stubborn as her mother, Molly kicked
back the covers and rose. She flung open the
door, pulled her mother off the doorstep and
into her room, ending her mother's public dis-
play of bad behavior. She smiled at her angry
landlord. "I'm sorry."

"I tried to send her away, but this woman is
determined," Lalalu said, hands on her bony
hips.

"I know. *Danke* for your efforts." Molly

waved a gentle goodbye, closed the door and then faced her mother. "What are you doing here?"

Ulla paced around the tiny room, agitation in her steps, her mouth slashed in an angry line. She spun toward her daughter. "*Ya*, just as I suspected. You've lost your sense of reason. You chose this room and that horrible *Englischer* woman over your wonderful bedroom at home...and me?"

Molly held her *mamm*'s gaze. "*Ya*, I did, *Mamm*. I chose this place, and Lalalu happens to be a very giving person. She's made me feel welcome here. This room is *my* home now. While I lived in your home, I showed you respect. Now I require as much from you."

Molly stood her ground, shoulders back, her mind screaming, *Help me, Gott.* Determined to ignore her *mamm*'s barbs, she pulled her robe over her nightgown and began to boil water for a mug of tea. She needed something to do while waiting for her mother's fury to end.

"It makes me wonder. Why have you shown this disrespect to me now? Since your *daed* passed, I have tried my best to be a *gut mamm* to you, but no. You would not let me be kind and loving."

"Don't bring *Daed* into this conversation.

This is about you and me and the demands you make in my life. Leave *Daed* at peace in his grave." Her voice broke, tears swimming in her eyes. Her *daed* had been too gentle a person to hold her *mamm* in check. They'd all suffered the consequences of her mother's harsh tongue.

"Your *daed* would be ashamed and disappointed in you." Ulla threw the hurtful words at Molly, her eyes dark with anger. "You choose to be…like this. You are Amish. It is time you behave like a young Amish girl and not abandon your moral and spiritual values." Ulla kicked at the ugly tile floor underfoot. "I blame that boss of yours at the café. She has been an evil influence in your life, that *Englischer* woman with her fancy ways."

Molly turned away from her mother, toward the screeching teakettle. She wiped tears from her face with the back of her hand before she poured boiling water over the tea bag. "Now you blame Willa Mae? Perhaps you're right, *Mamm*. Maybe she did help me grow up, become an independent woman. If what you say is true, then I must remember to tell her *danke*."

Ulla waved at the door. "You come home with me now, or I will report your irresponsible behavior." Ulla's eyes grew large, threatening. "Bishop Fischer will bring the *bann* down on you at my request. You need your job as community midwife to support yourself and this—" she threw her arms up in the air "—room you call a home. You'll have no place to stay on your miserable café tips and wages. This room will disappear, and so will your rebellion." Her *mamm* smiled, but there was no joy in the smile. Only anger.

"Do what you must. I have no intention of going back with you today."

"You want independence, a home of your own so badly? *Gut*, all this can be resolved by a quick marriage to Samuel. I've worked hard trying to find a suitable husband for you, someone who will put up with these willful ways of yours."

"*Ya*, you had me on the selling block, along with your jars of peaches and jams. You'd sell me to the highest bidder. Why can't you understand? I'm not ready for marriage. Why would I want to wed? I'd be replacing you with a bossy husband telling me when to eat, how to dress. What do I need with a husband? I have you to bully me."

Ulla walked toward her daughter, her fists

clenched. "Thank *Gott* your sister was different. Greta never gave me a moment's trouble. She followed rules, showed respect to me and your *daed*. You were always jealous of Greta's successful marriage, weren't you? It was Mose you wanted all along, but you waited too long. Now he has Sarah. You must look elsewhere."

Molly forced back the wave of tears that threatened to overwhelm her. "You're wrong, *Mamm*. I was never jealous of Greta's joy. Besides, Mose is like a big *bruder* to me. He was my dead sister's husband. It was your plan that I should marry him when Greta died, not mine. I would have never gone along with that. I loved my sister. You know I did. She was a kind and gentle person, like *Daed*. Greta never had to push for her rights. You gave them to her, allowed her to grow up and gave her so much more than me, things I never got. Like love."

Color high in her cheeks, Ulla slammed her fist on the counter and rattled Molly's tea mug. "I don't know what you're talking about. I treated both of you with the same love and respect." Her eyes grew red and watered. "Greta was easier to raise, less difficult."

"She was the pretty one, the one who pleased you. I always knew I was second best, the one to cook and clean, but never good enough to cherish."

"You are a foolish girl, full of yourself and pride. *Gott* will punish you for this rebellious spirit."

"I want you to leave now." Molly pointed to the door, her face set in angry lines.

Ulla walked to the door, held the knob in hand as she threw her words over her shoulder. "I'm serious, Molly. I *will* speak to Otto and the elders. He will follow the laws of the Ordnung. You will be unchurched." Ulla's eyes narrowed, her face pinched. "Is your freedom that important to you?"

Molly glared at her, her heart breaking. She fought to hold back the flood of tears she felt coming.

Ulla's arm raised as if to strike Molly, and then it fell to her side. "This decision is yours."

"Go!" Molly said in a firm, but quiet voice and then cringed when her mother slammed the door behind her. What had she done?

She punched Isaac's number into her cell phone and trembled as she waited for him to pick up.

Molly grimaced as she spoke. "There's big trouble. *Mamm* just left, and she's angrier than I've ever seen her. I think I might have made a mistake moving out. She's threatening to have me shunned." Her voice wobbled as she spoke the words.

"Do you think she'd do it?"

"*Ya*, sure she would." Molly wiped a tear from her cheek. She heard Isaac take in a deep breath. She shouldn't be bothering him with is, but she didn't know who else to reach out to who would understand.

"Do you think Mose and Sarah would let you move in with them for a while?"

"*Ya*, I hate to burden Sarah, but she could use my help when the baby comes. Still, that won't stop *Mamm*. She's relentless when it comes to getting her way."

"We'll see about that."

Chapter Twelve

Molly stirred in bed, then rose up on one elbow, her eyes blinking, not fully awake. Had someone called her name? She glanced around the pink bedroom. Where was she? Why was she in a child's room full of books and fluffy pink teddy bears and not in her tiny apartment? Then she remembered—Isaac lived in the tiny apartment now, and this was Beatrice and Mercy's room. The children had been shifted elsewhere in the house when she'd moved into Mose and Sarah's home the night before.

Guilt roiled her stomach. She'd managed to pull Isaac into her drama again, fool that she was. She should have refused his offer to take over her apartment and taken responsibility for her own actions. But no. She'd allowed herself to be rescued again. The poor man. What must he think of her?

"Are you awake, Aunt Molly?"

She looked in the direction of the small voice. Mercy stood at the foot of the bed, dressed in a long white nightgown, egg yolk smeared across one cheek, her blond hair a riot of untamed curls. Molly smiled at her younger niece. "*Ya,* I'm awake, *liebling. Gut mariye.*"

Hopping on one leg, Mercy grinned shyly and said, "*Mamm* said wake up, or no pancakes for you." Picking up the hem of her long gown, the little girl ran out of the room, slamming the door behind her.

Molly threw back the covers and placed her bare feet on the cool wooden floor. She stifled an enormous yawn with her hand as she rose. She didn't want to do anything but hide her head under the covers and go back to sleep, but years of self-control had her tidying the tossed bedsheets and quilt moments later. She'd had a restless night of disturbing dreams, but faced a busy day at the café, with no letup until seven, if she was lucky. She needed the distraction of a busy day to keep her from thinking about her life, her recent mistakes.

Beatrice met her coming down the hall, her

faceless doll tucked under her arm. "*Mamm*'s waiting on you."

"*Ya*, Mercy told me," Molly said, picking up the girl and laughing at her squeals of delight as she marched her into the kitchen. "I have a captive. Anyone want her?"

Sarah smiled. "*Gut mariye*. Did you sleep well?"

Molly shrugged. "Well enough." She patted Beatrice on the back and slid her down to the floor and then greeted Levi with a hug and kiss. "What a lovely boy. He's grown so tall. You must be so proud of him."

Two steaming pancakes were lifted off the grill and onto a plate for Molly. Sarah nodded and smiled. "We are proud of him, even when he dumps bugs on the floor and can't understand why he has to take them back outside."

"*Danke,*" Molly said, taking the pancakes. She pulled out a chair at the huge wooden table and sat, reaching for the warm maple syrup just out of reach. "I'd imagine the girls find a brother interesting to have around."

"You have no idea, but you will now that you're staying here," Sarah said with a laugh as she sat across from her. "Beatrice has had her fill of him already. She says he's a gross little boy with no manners and refuses to play with him, but Mercy has no problem with the bug-filled dump trucks he pushes around."

Molly took a bite of her pancakes and groaned with pleasure. "You really should open up a restaurant. These pancakes are wonderful."

"And when would I have time for this wonderful dream? Between diaper changes and dirty hands?" She grinned and then added, "But right now we need to talk about you, not me." She took Molly's hand and squeezed. "Tell me what's going on."

Closing the shop an hour early two days later, Isaac enjoyed the breeze blowing leaves at his feet and ruffling his hair. His leg hurt less, allowing him to leave the cane behind. He strolled by Molly's side, glad she'd accepted his invitation to go to the park and enjoy the warmth of the late-afternoon sun.

The twang of fiddles from Willie Burgess's Bluegrass Band could be heard all the way down to Gilbert Avenue. They crossed Pinecraft Park and finally drew close to the crowd of Amish, Mennonite and *Englischers* already seated in Birky Square on quilts, blankets and fold-out chairs.

Isaac's eyes searched for a patch of ground

for him and Molly to settle on, the homemade quilt folded across his arm, along with a wicker basket of food Molly had put together at the café. The outing was supposed to be a way to keep the rumors of their courtship going, but they had decisions to make. The situation was getting out of hand.

Molly tugged at Isaac's shirtsleeve and got his attention. She motioned toward a bare spot under a huge tree draped with strands of Spanish moss and grinned as he nodded in agreement.

He hesitated and then grabbed her warm hand, pushing her through a swarm of *Englischers* toe-tapping to the lively music all around them. Laughing at Molly's pleased expression, Isaac flipped out the colorful log cabin quilt and placed the basket of food in the middle of the colorful squares.

"This spot is perfect. We can see the stage from here," Molly shouted over the music.

"Don't break your arm patting yourself on the back," Isaac shouted back.

"You're terrible," she said without malice, and smiled. She held his gaze for a heartbeat and then began to glance around. "I didn't expect so many people to show up with this blast of cool air blowing in from the north."

He watched her settle on the quilt and was surprised to see her pat the spot next to her. "Come join me." Her expression was calm and inviting, no doubt an act to convince those around them that they were a courting couple. She was playing the part of a woman in love.

He favored his leg as he lowered himself, but made sure he was close enough to her to be convincing. "This is nice," he said, and wished he hadn't. They weren't really courting, after all. Only pretending.

He had been instructed by her to be attentive when people were around, but he was finding it hard to follow the plan, pretend to love her only when it was necessary. The more time he spent with her, the more he realized he had begun to have real feelings for her. He longed to leave his past behind him and make this courtship real, but his common sense told him not to be foolish. His baggage from the past had to be dealt with. Until then he had nothing to offer her but his own brand of misery and hardship. He couldn't press for a real relationship with her, even if by some chance she might come to care about him in the future.

Molly laughed out loud as a Mennonite couple strolled past, pushing a small boy in a red wagon with wooden slates. "He looks like he's having a good time," she said, glancing at Isaac. Her foot tapped out the beat of the song being played, her cheeks glowing pink from the brisk, cool air.

"Maybe you should have brought a jacket," Isaac mentioned, seeing her rub her hands together from the cold. "This cold front has a sharper bite than forecasted."

She began to dig into the basket, withdrawing plastic containers full of his favorite food and placing them on the quilt within reach. "*Nee*, I'm good. If I get cold, we can always snuggle," she said and leaned against him for seconds, her words casual, her smile innocent and teasing. "You hungry yet?"

"That's a silly question." Isaac grabbed the paper plate she held out. He added two golden-brown chicken legs to a pile of German potato salad and dropped a sour pickle in the middle of the feast. "This food looks wonderful. Did you cook it?"

Molly took a generous bite of her corn on the cob. "*Nee*, Willa Mae cooked it special, just for you."

"That was nice of her," Isaac said around a forkful of creamy potato salad.

"She's one of the nicest women I know."

"She knows about our ruse?" Isaac wondered out loud.

"*Ya*, and she's all right with it, but she says you're too nice for your own good. That's why she fried the chicken and made potato salad for you. She knows it's something you order at the café and wanted to make the meal special for you. It's her way of saying thanks for helping out."

"That was nice of her, but not necessary." He expressed his gratitude by biting into a crunchy chicken leg.

"I know, but you're a kind and loyal friend. You deserve special treats."

Isaac looked down at his plate and moved his food around, his appetite suddenly gone. Molly's comment made him sound more like a faithful family dog than a suitor.

The musicians took a break, and people began to mill around, chatting in groups. Mothers cleared up their picnic spots, called to children playing close by. Isaac took the whoopie pie Molly handed him and placed it on his plate of half-eaten food.

"Something wrong?" Molly asked, her gaze searching his face.

Isaac shook his head. "I guess I'm not as hungry as I thought." He'd been pretending about a lot of things lately. The idea of a fake courtship didn't set well with him anymore. They were spending a lot of time together, and he realized he longed for her attention to be real, not pretend. Not a day went by that someone didn't ask him, "When's the wedding?" He found himself wanting to answer, "Christmas," but couldn't. Conviction ate at him. He knew the truth was always more profitable than a lie, but he couldn't let Molly down. Not when she needed him most.

Twilight brought a new round of people to the park and seemed to scatter the family folk with young children. Young *Englischers* walked the paths with their fingers intertwined, stopping to hug or steal a kiss. Molly watched Isaac talking with a couple of men from the church a few feet away. He looked handsome in his new blue shirt and black suspenders. She'd made the shirt herself, with Sarah's help. She'd even sewed snaps down the front, something she'd never been able to do before. He'd been so surprised when she'd presented her gift to him. She got the impression he hadn't received many presents in his life. She had no idea what his childhood had been like, if he had a good family, or if he had a good relationship with them. He never spoke of family back home. Someone named Rose was connected to him in some way, but Molly didn't let herself dwell on the woman. It was none of her business.

Echoes of her fight with her mother came back, stealing her joy. She'd only seen her *mamm* once since she'd asked her to leave her home. The day before, Ulla had been with Samuel Bawell at the café, their heads close together, as if plotting some new scheme to pull Molly back into their world. She fought down her anger and busied herself with clearing up the leftover food, determined not to let her mother's controlling behavior spoil her time with Isaac.

The band left for the night, and a few choir members sang gospel songs. The crunch of freshly fallen leaves made her glance to her side. Samuel Bawell stood there looking down at her, his feet just off the quilt, his smile bright.

"I didn't see you at choir practice. How have you been?"

"I'm *gut*. Just busy. And you?" Molly said, trying to be friendly without giving him false hope. There was no telling what her mother had told him about his chances with her.

"Oh, I've been fine, just fine." He tugged at his collar and snapped it closed. "I went wind sailing yesterday with some friends. It was quite the experience." He grinned, flashing sparkling white teeth. "I wish you had been there. I left a message for you at your job. I miss our time together."

"I was busy with work. I really didn't have time for answering messages or playing sports." Molly straightened her *kapp*.

"You'd have time for lots of things if you stopped resisting and married me."

His words hang in the air.

"Your *mamm* told me you've moved out. The bishop can't be happy with your actions. He's bound to call you in for counsel. Your reputation could easily be sullied."

"It's none of your business where I live or what I do, Samuel. We've had this conversation before. You know I don't love—" Molly began, only to have her words cut off by Samuel.

"*Ya*, I know you say you don't love me, but I'm not giving up, Molly. I love you. Have for years. You know that. I want to provide you with all the things you deserve. You could have a wonderful life with me. A big home, our children would want for nothing. Your *mamm*'s already said she's prepared to leave Pinecraft and come with us to Ohio if you're worried about being lonely."

Molly shook her head, exasperated.

"What could possibly stand in our way?"

"I could," Isaac said as he wandered over and placed a protective hand on Molly's shoulder. "Molly's not interested in you or your money. She doesn't need you."

Molly watched Samuel's gaze become intense. "And what can you offer her, Isaac Graber? Financial struggles for the rest of her life? Your children starving on your store's meager income? Is that really how you want her to live? Hand-to-mouth, wondering where the next meal is coming from? I can offer her so much more, and I have her mother's blessing. Why don't you step aside for Molly's sake? Do the right thing."

Molly rose from the quilt and stood next to Isaac, her arm going around his slim waist. "I think it's time you went your way, Samuel. Isaac and I are courting now, making plans for a Christmas wedding. I'm an adult. I don't need my mother's blessing to be wed." She took a deep breath and continued speaking as she walked up to Samuel. "And how Isaac and I manage financially is none of your business. Money isn't everything. Love is. You can tell that bit of news to my interfering *mamm*."

"I understand you're infatuated with him, Molly, but if you change your mind—"

"I won't change my mind. Isaac is a good man, who's loyal and honest. I love him. I once thought you were a nice man, too, but you're not. You're spoiled. You think only of yourself, the better things in life. And you're a bully, Samuel Bawell. Now go! Get out of here before I report *you* to Bishop Fischer. I think he'd be interested in knowing the way you've tried to intimidate me and push your way into my life." Molly motioned toward the path and repeated, "Go!"

Molly watched Samuel walk away. She didn't start to tremble until seconds later when she realized what she'd done. She'd placed Isaac in a very difficult position. Their pretend courtship could have easily been explained away when Samuel left Pinecraft if she'd only kept her mouth shut about love and a wedding date.

She and Isaac could have stopped seeing each other, told their friends the courtship didn't work out and that would have been the end of the farce. But her words of love for Isaac and comments on an upcoming Christmas wedding had firmly cemented them into a real relationship.

If Samuel repeated her declaration of their

upcoming marriage to anyone, especially her *mamm*, her lie would have far-reaching repercussions and would be more difficult to explain away.

Molly dropped her head to her chest. Isaac hadn't bargained on anything more than a pretend courtship that might last a few weeks at best. Her lie was a sin, and she'd caused Isaac to sin by the act of omission.

Isaac deserved better than this. He'd become a good friend and tried to help. Now she'd paid him back for his generosity with lies. Lies that only she could set straight. Now they would have to go to the bishop and explain. She'd have to confess and ask for forgiveness, and hope that Isaac would be able to forgive her, too.

Chapter Thirteen

Ten minutes of waiting in Otto Fischer's office the next day had Isaac's stomach churning. His heart racing. What would happen now? He thought about the shop, and Mose's inexperienced nephew who was filling in for him.

He leaned forward and glanced at Molly. She sat straight and prim in a wooden chair next to her brother-in-law, Mose. Her pale blue dress accentuated the color of her fair skin and hair, making her lovelier than he had ever seen her.

Isaac smiled, trying to reassure her, but her brown eyes quickly darted away and focused on her hands. Her fingers continued to tear at the tissue he'd given her moments before.

The door opened and the bishop walked in, bringing with him the fragrant aroma of chicken pot pie, no doubt his noontime meal.

He looked around the room, his sharp blue eyes taking in first Molly and Isaac, and then his son, Mose. Pulling out a chair, he made himself comfortable behind his desk. "I hear I have a bit of bother to concern myself with instead of eating rhubarb compote and sponge cake under my shade trees."

Mose cleared his throat, as if to speak, but Molly jumped up and spoke first. "I have sinned and drawn Isaac Graber into my foolishness, Bishop Fischer."

Isaac watched her every move. He noticed her hands trembling at her sides. His heart went out to her. He stood, not willing to let her take all the blame. He'd been at fault, too. He could have stopped seeing Molly, ended the game. Instead, he'd pretended their courtship was real. He wouldn't let her face this situation alone. Not while he had breath in his body. "We both have sinned," he stated.

Molly turned toward him, her face creased in frustration. "Isaac, please sit down! You've already done enough. I won't have you taking my blame as your own. We both know—"

Otto banged his empty coffee mug like a gavel. "Perhaps you both could sit down and give me a chance to ask a few questions. I'll decide who's at fault here and who's not."

Isaac felt like a reprimanded child. He dropped into his chair and rubbed the side of his bad leg.

Molly slowly took her seat and tucked her feet under her chair. She glared at Isaac and then glanced back at Otto, who waited patiently behind his desk.

Mose stood. "I don't think this will take long, *Daed*. Molly and Isaac have a problem regarding Ulla. They spoke to me today, and I suggested they come to you for counsel. We're hoping you can unravel this situation with as little repercussion as possible."

Otto stroked his beard, his forehead creasing. "Ulla, huh. What has she done this time?" He turned toward Molly, his lips curved into a sympathetic smile. "Speak up, child."

"Ah…you see. Oh, there is no way to make this story short, Bishop." Molly let her chin fall to her chest and used what was left of her tissue to dab at her eyes.

"I'm here, Molly. Let me help. My job is to lead and direct the good people of this community. Judgment comes from the Lord, not from me."

She lifted her chin. "My *mamm* and I have a difference of opinion. She wants me to marry Samuel Bawell. I told her I wouldn't under any circumstances. I'm twenty-one, not some *youngie* who doesn't know her own mind. She has no right to tell me who I can and cannot marry." She sucked in air and went on. "We quarreled and I got angry." She lowered her chin. "I moved out of my *mamm*'s home."

"I know your *mamm* can be—" Otto cleared his throat and seemed to choose his words carefully "—difficult when riled, but moving out on your own was not a prudent choice, Molly." He looked at her with an arched brow. "How long have you been living on your own?"

"Just a few days, *Daed*. Molly is staying with Sarah and me for now." Mose smiled as he informed his father of the news.

"*Gut, gut.* Go on, Molly."

"At Birky Square last night, Isaac and I were listening to music and Samuel Bawell…he, ah, he came over and asked me to marry him again. I turned him down, as I usually do. You see, my *mamm* gave him permission to marry me without my consent." She turned to Mose. "I don't want to marry Samuel. I never have. I don't love him, and I've told him so over and over. I got angry and spoke before I thought."

She shifted her gaze back to the bishop, her eyes glistening. "I told a lie, pure and simple." She sniffed and wiped at her nose. "I told Samuel that Isaac and I were courting, which wasn't true. We were only pretending to walk out together to keep *Mamm* out of my business." She dropped her head again. "Then I told Samuel that Isaac and I would be married by Christmas."

She shrugged. "I just wanted Samuel to go away and leave me alone, once and for all. Now I need *Gott*'s forgiveness and your help to get out of the mess I've created."

Molly drew in another deep breath and glanced at Isaac. "All Isaac did was go along with the pretense in order to help me. He didn't mean to sin. It was me," she said, her voice rough and high. "He's not at fault. I was the one—"

"*Ya*, so you said, Molly, but I still see Isaac as complicit in this matter." Otto turned toward Isaac. "He could have spoken up, corrected you."

Isaac nodded. "*Ya*, I could have, but I didn't."

Turning back toward Molly, Otto said, "I assume the news is out and Ulla knows about the impending wedding?" He rubbed his chin, pulling at his full beard as he waited for her response.

"I think so. I feel sure Samuel has told her and anyone else who'd listen. He was very angry when he left the park." Molly mopped the tears from her eyes.

Otto shifted his gaze back to Isaac. "You were there when Molly told this lie, and yet you kept silent. Why is that?"

Isaac nodded. "I didn't just keep silent. I added to the lie." Isaac felt his face heat with emotion. "The man's ego is as large as his bankbook. I lost my temper. I didn't care if I became a part of the lie. I just wanted him to leave Molly alone."

Leaning forward in his chair, Otto tapped his fingers on the surface of his desk and pondered the situation for long moments. "Obviously you two are fond of each other, even protective." He glanced at both of them and flashed a quick smile. "It wonders me. Perhaps the way to correct this lie is by making the lie become truth. There's nothing wrong with an arranged marriage once in a while, even though it's not as popular among *youngies* as it once was. Sometimes arranged marriages are for the best."

Otto's smile reappeared, but broader now. "My parents picked my bride, and I've been a happy man for many years. Theda has proven to be my right arm, a real blessing in my life. I would hate to live without her wisdom and help.

Your union can be the same, if you work at it. You said the wedding is to be in December?"

Molly nodded. "But—"

"Christmas weddings are the loveliest, though my schedule is already full. We'll work something out for you and Isaac," Otto remarked and then added, "Ulla will come 'round. You'll see. She'll want to be part of the planning and probably take over the arrangements." He laughed out loud, amusing himself.

Molly jumped up, her eyes large and round. She took a deep breath. "Bishop, you don't understand. We didn't mean for it to go this far. Isaac has no interest in marriage to anyone, especially to me, and I—"

Isaac stood with her, directed his gaze at Otto. He had to do something and fast. "You know better than most that the bike shop is struggling financially. If we married, I'd have nothing to offer Molly in the way of comfort or security." He struggled for breath, not sure what to say. If he didn't have his past to deal with, he would gladly agree to marry Molly under any circumstances, but not like this, with Otto forcing her hand. "I can't expect Molly to venture into a marriage without some security."

"This marriage solution is far better than her being unchurched, and that's how it will end if her *mamm* has anything to say about it, and you know she will. She'll stir the community into a frenzy, force my hand and ruin your name."

He looked at Molly, and she dropped her head again. "I'm sure you two will figure it all out, just like Theda and I did. We lived on cabbage and salt pork and received help from the community for the first two years of our marriage."

His gaze shifted to Isaac. "Theda never complained, and I'm sure Molly won't, either. We have a happy marriage and lots of rosy-cheeked grandchildren. You both can have this, too. Sometimes it's these impromptu moments in life that are the most fun. You'll see."

Molly sliced a desperate look Isaac's way and then turned back to Otto. "If only you'd—"

"There's no need to thank me, child. I'll announce the banns this coming Sunday morning. That should bring you peace with *Gott* and keep Ulla out of your hair for a while." Otto rose. "Now, it's time for my snack under the trees. Mose, show these two lovebirds out."

As they walked away from Otto Fischer's home a small rock in the road caused Molly to stumble. Isaac grabbed for her arm and steadied her.

"Danke," she said, not looking at him. She was too embarrassed. What had just transpired was all her fault, and she'd firmly wedged Isaac in the middle of her mess.

She put one foot in front of the other, praying. Isaac was very quiet. Too quiet. She could only imagine what he was thinking, how he felt about being put in this kind of situation. He had no interest in marriage. He'd said as much in the meeting they'd just left. She glanced up at him. His face was hidden under the shadow of his black wool hat. *What is he thinking?* Was he concentrating on ways to get himself out of this predicament?

Isaac eased closer and asked, "Do you have a shift at the café today?"

"Nee. Willa Mae gave me the morning off. Why?"

"Gut. I thought we could…" He held down his hat as a brisk wind blew. "Perhaps you'd like to go to the park. Talk about things in private. There are things I need to tell you."

Molly pulled at the ribbon dancing against her neck. *"Ya*, okay."

Isaac took her arm as they waited for a cluster of bike riders to pass, then crossed the road leading to Pinecraft Park.

Fall leaves crunched underfoot as they made

their way across the sun-drenched park, to the old picnic table positioned by a slow-moving creek. Several tourists and an Amish family of six, with homemade fishing poles poked under their arms, strolled past, offered greetings and warm smiles.

Molly did her best to respond to their friendly gestures, but her heart wasn't in it. She'd created a monstrous situation, turned Isaac's life upside down. He'd been threatened with being shunned, his reputation ruined. He had to be furious with her. She didn't look forward to the talk they were about to have, not that she didn't deserve every ounce of his anger.

Birds scattered as the couple trudged toward the worn picnic table and settled themselves across from each other. Molly was out of breath from their fast march, her slightly shorter leg causing her hip to hurt. She ignored her discomfort and searched for a clean handkerchief from her dress pocket. Her nose was stuffed from crying in frustration. Her lie, spoken impulsively and meant to ward off problems, had done nothing but seriously complicate her life and now Isaac's.

Her fingers rummaged around and found the white square of soft cotton. She shook it out and then blew her nose hard. She sniffed. She had to look a mess, her eyes puffy and her nose red.

Isaac said nothing. He seemed to be waiting for her to compose herself.

"I hope you know how sorry I am for all this. I should have never asked for your help. Please forgive me," Molly muttered, shifting uncomfortably on the wooden bench. She glanced up, studied the frown on his face.

"You owe me no apology, Molly. Let's talk calmly and rationally for a minute," Isaac suggested. "Let's just wait a few days, let things settle. I might be able to persuade Bishop Fischer to change his mind about a December wedding."

Molly stood, her frustration palpable. "I want that, too, but how do we manage to convince him? You heard what he said."

"Please. Let me finish," he urged, and motioned for her to sit.

Molly had no idea what his plan was, but she sat, arranging her skirt around her legs.

"We're both in this situation. You stretched the truth. I stretched it, too."

"Yes, but you didn't mean—"

"It doesn't matter what either of us meant now. I don't know about you, but I'm not okay with being unchurched, and if the bishop won't listen, then marriage is the only way out of this." He frowned as he spoke. "We've already asked for *Gott*'s forgiveness, so let's keep pretending we're all for this coming marriage and then maybe, if you want, we can back out at the last moment. I'll do something terrible that will give you an out. No one will even suspect, except maybe Mose and Bishop Fischer."

Molly wiped a tear from her eye. "Give me an out? You must be joking, Isaac. We didn't just buy a car that won't run and want to return it. Our bishop has just arranged our marriage. The rest of our lives kind of marriage."

She grabbed his hand. "I believe marriage is a sacred commitment, something a person doesn't enter into lightly. How can we just *not* get married if the bishop announces our banns and insists we go through with the wedding?" She gazed into his eyes, trying to read his mood.

"*Ya,* I know marriage is serious business," he finally said.

She dabbed at her nose. "In the meeting you said your business is just starting out, not bringing in enough money to support a family." Her brows rose in question. "Not once did you mention anything about feeling love or commitment to me. If you meant to fool the bishop that you really do love me, you failed miserably." Her face flamed hot. She looked down and murmured, "I know you don't love me, but the bishop doesn't. Shouldn't he think you do?"

Isaac leaned forward at the mentioned of the word love. He reached for Molly's hand, but she pulled away, determined to end the conversation.

Molly's mind raced. She needed to get away from Isaac, to think calmly without his searching eyes watching her so intently. He wore a pained expression. "I think I need to go home now."

"If you'll just let me speak, I can explain my hesitation," Isaac said, reaching for her again.

"No. You and I have both said enough. I need to think. This is not the way I envisioned speaking to my future husband about our coming marriage. No woman wants to be trapped in a loveless marriage, and we both know that could happen if your plan doesn't work. All my life I dreamed of a hero who would snatch me up into his arms and carry me off because he loved me, not because Otto Fischer says he must. *Gott* has a man in mind for me, and you're not that man."

Chapter Fourteen

Days passed without contact from Isaac. Christmas was fast approaching.

Theda skirted past Molly on her way to the refrigerator in Sarah's kitchen. "Why not use the electric mixer, *schatzi*?" The older woman smiled, her eyes fixed on the bowl of limp egg whites Molly was endlessly whisking.

Molly paused, moving her arm back and forth, ready to give up. She'd been working on the egg whites for a good five minutes, but wasn't getting anywhere with them.

"We're going to need that meringue in a few minutes. The pie crusts are almost brown and it won't take long for them to cool."

"*Ya*, my mind was on other things." Her mind had been a million miles away, thinking about Isaac, how fast time was flying, and not about the pie contest and auction on the church grounds later that day. She'd have to face Isaac again this afternoon, and she wasn't looking forward to it. Not after their talk in the park. Molly reached under the counter, grabbed the hand mixer and plugged it in.

"I can imagine your mind is on other things," Sarah said, giving her a wink.

The past few days Sarah had been hinting that she knew about the December wedding fiasco. She'd even made celery soup last night and commented at the dinner table how hard it was to find good celery for weddings this time of year.

Molly slowly added sprinkles of sugar to the frothy egg mixture until she saw the beginnings of peaks and was able to rev up the mixer's motor and drown out her own thoughts.

After church service tomorrow, there would be no turning back. Everyone would know about her and Isaac's courtship.

They would be officially engaged.

The men would start teasing Isaac about the quickly arranged wedding. The woman at the Anabaptist church she and Isaac attended loved planning winter weddings. They'd organize the event, with or without her help, making sure her color choice was used on the tables. They'd be asking her questions she didn't have answers to, talking about things she didn't want to deal with.

She turned off the mixer. The egg whites had peaked to perfection, despite her neglect. With a push of her finger, the frothy beaters dropped into the tub of sudsy hot water in the sink. She wiped down the mixer with a clean cloth and mindlessly unplugged it.

Molly had always thought her wedding day would be the happiest time of her life, but she didn't feel happy. She felt trapped into another loveless marriage. And, if their lie did come out, everyone would think she was an old maid who'd had to trick a man into marriage.

"Why so glum? You've always loved pie contests." Theda put her arms around Molly's shoulders and hugged her.

Tears began to swim in Molly's eyes. All she did was cry lately. She looked at Theda and saw compassion and understanding on the older woman's face. Molly broke down, tears flowing, holding on to Theda like a drowning child.

"That's right, *liebling*. You cry it out. Tell us how we can help," Theda said, patting her back.

"No one can help," Molly sobbed.

Sarah tore off a piece of paper towel and

pressed it into Molly's hand. "Don't cry about the wedding. Everything will work out. You'll see."

Molly looked at Sarah. "You already know about the lie?"

Sarah nodded. "*Ya*, I know. We both do. Our husbands can't keep secrets from us." She grinned. "You'll see. Isaac will find it hard to keep secrets from you, too."

Theda led Molly to a kitchen chair and pulled one out for herself. "This wedding isn't the end of the world, *liebling*. Both Sarah and I started out our marriages on rocky ground, but look at us now. We're happy, our men content. So what if you told a lie to an unwanted suitor?" She put her hands on Molly's shoulders. "I might have done the same in your shoes. You've been forgiven by *Gott*, haven't you? He understands you and Isaac meant no real harm. *Gott*'s not punishing you. You're punishing yourself by thinking this arranged marriage is wrong and that *Gott* is not in it."

"But Isaac—" Molly moaned.

"Forget about Isaac. He's a man. He doesn't know what he wants. Time will bring him around," Theda assured her, patting Molly on the arm.

"He did nothing but help me, and it got him into this mess. He didn't once mention he loved me when we talked," Molly sobbed, tears rolling down her cheeks.

"I wouldn't be so sure of that. I've seen how he looks at you when he thinks no one is watching," Sarah said. "Come on. Dry your tears, tidy yourself. Let's go to the church and help the ladies set up for the contest. Forget all of this for now. You have to trust in *Gott*'s will for your life."

Pedaling as fast as he could with a sore leg, Isaac rode through the empty streets of Pinecraft, his thoughts on what was facing him. Otto's wife had asked him to be one of the pie contest judges, but Molly would be there. They hadn't talked since she'd hurried away from the park days before, leaving him alone with his confused thoughts. He had no idea how she felt about their situation now that she'd had time to think.

At the side of the church, Isaac parked his bike, then dusted off the bottom of his black trousers before walking to the back lawn of the church.

Men were busy setting up tables, the women arranging chairs. Mose motioned for Isaac to join him. He ambled over, glancing around to see if he could find Molly. She was nowhere in sight, but he spotted Sarah and the children close by. Throwing his jacket across the back of a chair, Isaac lifted the other end of the table Mose was moving.

"*Gott* has given us a beautiful day, *ya*?" Mose said, walking backward toward several rows of tables close by.

"*Ya,*" Isaac responded, pulling out a set of metal legs and helping to turn the table over.

"*Mamm* tells me she bullied you into being a judge."

Lifting another table, Isaac grinned at Mose. "She did. She's quite formidable for someone so small and fragile. She said it was my civic duty as a Pinecraft shop owner."

Mose laughed. "She used the same argument on me. Next year I'm not going to fall for her fresh apple pie and 'let's have a little talk.'"

"At least you got pie. I got an earful of 'loyalty to Pinecraft.' She even sent her grandson to the shop to fill in for me so I'd be free to judge." Isaac pulled out another set of legs at his end of the next table, and together the two men finished the last setup.

"Come on. Let's get something to drink before one of the women comes up with another job for us," Mose said, a twinkle in his eyes.

In a pink dress that made her cheeks look

rosy, Molly stood behind the drinks table, wispy strands of hair blowing around her *kapp*, a bright smile on her face. She looked his way. Her smiled died a sudden death.

"Sweet tea or lemonade?" she asked Mose.

"Tea with extra ice," he said. "You look very nice today. Is that a new dress?"

"*Ya, danke.* I made it, with Sarah's help." She busied herself, adding more ice to his glass.

"You did a great job. Someday your husband will be proud of your money-saving talents," Mose said with a smile and stepped aside.

"Tea or lemonade?" Molly asked Isaac, her lips curved, but her eyes were not smiling.

"Lemonade, *bitte.*" Isaac took the glass she handed him and leaned in close. "Could we eat together later, after the pie contest?"

"I've got lots to do, Isaac. I'm not sure I'll have time for a meal."

"But we really need to talk," he murmured softly.

"*Ya,* we do, maybe later," Molly returned, ignoring him as she waited on the next person in line.

Mose put his arm around Isaac's shoulders and spoke to him like an older brother as they strode away. "Don't be discouraged. Women are strange but delightful creatures. They either love you or find you unbearably distasteful, and that can be in a single day." He laughed ruefully and downed the last of his tea in one long gulp.

Isaac watched Molly laugh out loud at something a beardless Amish man said. Jealousy ate at him. He wanted her to be that relaxed around him, show him the better side of her like she used to do, before the lie. He turned his head toward Mose. "*Ya*, I'm constantly in and out of hot water with Molly, and most of the time I have no idea why."

"My *daed* gave me some good advice years ago. He said, 'treat your wife with dignity and respect. Show your love in actions, not words.' I find it doesn't hurt if you make sure you come home while the food's still hot on the table, too. Use *Daed*'s bit of advice, and I can guarantee you'll always have a happy wife and kids."

"Kids?" Isaac hadn't thought about having *kinner*. If he and Molly did marry, children would be the natural result of their union. Was he ready to be a father? What if he became an angry, bitter old man like his own father? But then, he knew he didn't have to worry about children. Once Molly heard about his past, she'd break the engagement, finish with him for good. No one would blame her.

"Don't look so scared. *Kinner* are wonderful blessings from *Gott*. I can't wait for our next one to get here."

"But the responsibilities and money it takes to run a family... How do you handle the stress?"

Mose sat on a bench and made room for Isaac. "It's easy. I take each day as it comes and give all my concerns to *Gott*. He does the rest. He will for you, too."

"Molly doesn't love me." Isaac bowed his head, ashamed to be saying the hard, cruel facts out loud.

"Oh, I think she does. I know Molly. She wouldn't be letting *Daed* or her *mamm* put her in this situation if she didn't want to get married. The Molly I know is smart and resourceful. If she wanted out of this marriage arrangement, you'd be the first to know. Believe me. Deep down Molly has to know *Daed* wouldn't unchurch her over a lie, even if it is a big one." Mose looked at him and laughed. "*Nee*, not his Molly. She's like his own child."

"But why has she allowed Ulla to bully her into this rash decision?"

"Because deep down, Molly wants to marry you, *bensel*. Think about it."

Isaac sighed. He didn't know what to think.

All he knew for sure was that his feelings for Molly had suddenly grown into something more powerful than his guilt about the past, or concern about his poverty. He was prepared to tell her about Thomas. He had to set the record straight, and today was as good a day as any. "*Ya*, you may be right. Maybe she does have feelings for me."

"Have you told her how you feel?"

"*Nee*. Not yet." Isaac rubbed his hands down his thighs, his stomach in a twist. "But I will."

All her chores done and too tired to care who won the pie contest, Molly gathered her belongings and crossed the church lawn, stopping only to bend and pat the old church cat who lived under the tool shed.

"Hello, kitty. You like your neck scratched? *Ya,* it's *gut*." Silky soft, the adult cat began to purr and lean its body into her fingers.

"So you sneak away like a thief in the night."

Molly didn't have to turn. She knew who was speaking loud enough for everyone to hear. She stood and turned, facing her mother, not prepared to do battle in front of the whole church, but not in the mood to be mocked, either. "*Nee, Mamm*. Not sneaking away. Just going home. It's been a long day. I'm tired."

Dressed in a pale shade of blue, Ulla looked like she'd made an effort with her appearance today, something she seldom did. Her *kapp* was perfectly positioned, her dress starched and crisply pressed. "I see Isaac has already abandoned you. Too bad you didn't listen to your *mamm* about Samuel. He would never have left you to walk home alone."

She looked directly into her mother's eyes and spoke softly. "*Ya,* I know. Samuel is perfect. I've heard it a thousand times. I just don't happen to love Samuel. Doesn't that matter to you at all?"

"Is it a sin for a mother to want what is best for her younger daughter? *Nee,* I think not." Ulla tugged at Molly's arm, almost shaking her off balance.

Molly sighed. "What's best for me is—"

"You are too young to know what is best for you. You've proven that with your foolish choices. What has Isaac Graber got that Samuel didn't have? Samuel has money, a strong position in the community. Isaac has a run-down shop and no future here in Pinecraft. I've made a good match for you, but you whine about the foolishness of love. It's your financial future you should be most concerned about."

"Didn't you love *Daed* when you married him?" Molly jerked her arm away.

"Your father." Ulla laughed, her words grating. *"Nee*, I didn't love him. Not for one moment. He was weak and dull, even as a young man. I wed to get out of my parents' *haus*, to have freedom, but all I got was hard work and children."

"But *Daed* loved you," Molly declared, her voice rising slightly. "He worked until the day he died providing for us."

"Ya, well, that he did, but it wasn't enough. He and I struggled our whole life, and when he died he left me penniless, and I continued to struggle to support you and your sister. Do you know how it will feel to have to rely on the community for food?" Ulla leaned in, her voice lowered. "That's why I've been courting John. I'm going to marry him. There will be no more leaning on people who whisper behind my back and gossip."

Ulla lifted her hands, as if to shove Molly away. "But go your own path. Find this foolish love that brings you so much happiness. As for me, I will do as I always do. Take care of myself." Ulla turned and walked through the cluster of muttering onlookers, her back straight and proud.

Molly felt strong arms slip around her shoulders and turned to find Isaac, his face etched in anger as he watched her mother stride away.

Chapter Fifteen

Isaac lowered himself, sitting on the same deck step as Molly. He watched as she dug her toes into the green grass underfoot, her flip-flops tossed to one side. Today was the first time he'd seen her tiny feet bare. She always wore black dress shoes with thin stockings. He suspected the pale pink nail polish on the tips of her toes had something to do with her niece Beatrice.

Molly turned toward him, her face still blotchy from all the crying she'd done as they walked back to Mose and Sarah's house together after the pie contest.

"I'm always saying *danke* to you, Isaac," she murmured, her voice low, the wind catching her words of apology and carrying them away.

"What are you thanking me for now?"

She surprised him when she rested her head

on his shoulder for a few moments and then whispered, "For putting up with all the drama. For being there when I need you most." She took a deep breath, gave him a watery grin and then looked away. "I'm sorry you had to deal with my wailing. All I seem to do lately is cry like a fool. You must have been embarrassed with all those people walking past, gawking at me."

"I have to admit it's not every day I walk down the street with a sobbing woman on my arm, but for you, anything." He grinned at her, but her chin was down again, her shoulders slumped.

"We have to have a serious talk." Molly sat upright, her voice hoarse from crying. She shielded her eyes from the sun shining through the tree's canopy overhead. "We can't allow the banns to be announced tomorrow." Scooting closer, her expression turned hopeful. "Perhaps you should try and talk to Bishop Fischer again, convince him you have no interest in marriage, especially to me. I would completely understand if you told him I was an unfit woman, not the kind you want to tie yourself to. He'd probably have something to say, but isn't getting lectured better than a marriage you don't want?"

"I could try to talk to him, but I've grown

kind of fond of the idea of marrying you." He shoved back the bill of his black wool hat and pretended to write in the air. "Mrs. Isaac Graber. It has a nice ring... Don't you think?"

Molly twisted, her knees bumping his legs. "You can't be serious." Her dark eyes grew round with surprise.

"I am," Isaac proclaimed. "I'm very serious. I've been doing a lot of thinking. It's time I marry. I need a wife. Someone to do my laundry and cook my meals. I need to be practical." He smiled at her as he said the last sentence, but his stomach was in a ball of knots. He was stalling. He had to say the right words, how he really felt about her, about what he'd done to Thomas.

"Yes, but what about love and commitment? Are you willing to marry without love?"

"You seemed fond enough of me just a moment ago." His brow went up in a suggestive manner. "You just had your head on my shoulder, and that's an outrageous act for a woman who insists she's not courting me and says she feels no affection."

"We aren't courting," she declared and then amended her statement with a shake of her head. "Well, not really courting. It's all an act. You know it. I know it. You only agreed to help stave off Samuel's unwanted advances. Otherwise I would never have asked—"

"What? Asked me to court you?" He pushed his thumbs under his suspenders and snapped them. "I think I'm a pretty fair catch, considering the considerable lack of local young men to pick from."

"Has anyone ever told you that you're conceited, Isaac Graber?"

"Nope. You'd be the first." Isaac shrugged. "Why don't we just go along with the ruse, let the banns be read, continue to court each other and see what happens. You never know. We might end up—"

The back door flew open and Beatrice ran out onto the deck, shouting, "Aunt Molly, come quick! *Mamm's* having the baby."

Working on autopilot, Isaac managed to cook a bubbling pan of franks and beans and not burn the simple meal. He peeled three bananas and sliced them, chopped in a couple of apples and added a few walnuts chunks to the fruit salad.

A green grape tossed high in the air landed in his mouth. He chewed as he topped off the healthy dessert with the handful of the juicy green grapes.

"How long has it been now?"

Isaac placed three small plastic plates on the table and then answered Mose. "Five hours, but who's counting?"

Mose tied a handmade bib of terry cloth around Levi's chubby neck and kissed the little boy on his rosy cheek. "He wants his *mamm*. He's been crying for hours. Sarah would have a fit if she knew I was feeding the *kinner* this late in the evening, but—"

"You've been a bit busy, Mose. Don't be so hard on yourself. The *kinner* are strong. They won't die from eating cookies once in a while instead of a hot meal."

"Shh. Not so loud. Sarah might hear and come out of that bed. I know her. She's a stickler for routine and homemade meals." Mose smiled, but there was no joy in his grimace. Just worry.

"*Mamm* said our sister will be here soon," Beatrice declared, her excitement visible in her shining eyes and the toothy grin that exposed her first missing tooth.

"Did you sneak into that room again?" Mose demanded, his tone harsher than usual.

Beatrice shrugged. "Yes, but Mercy told me to do it. She wanted to see *Mamm*." She pointed at her younger sister and almost fell out of her chair trying to avoid her finger being bitten by her younger sister.

"You both went in?" Mose's brows rose.

"No, I only went in. Molly pushed me out the door."

"*Gut*, I'm glad she did. You must not bother your *mamm* right now. She and Molly are very busy, and they don't need *kinner* around." He turned toward his younger daughter and frowned. "Mercy, don't bite your sister. We've talked about this many times. You must be a *gut* girl."

Mercy's face puckered, preparing for a boisterous wail.

Mose dropped into the chair next to Levi and spooned food into the baby's mouth as he thundered, "Enough, both of you." He wiped Levi's face with a napkin and lowered his voice. "Eat your meal."

Isaac stuck a forkful of beans in his mouth and chewed. *So, this is what it's like to be a* daed. No wonder his own father often walked the back acres of their farm. Probably to get away from his own *kinner.*

He grinned as Beatrice glanced over at him, her mouth bulging with fresh fruit, a twinkle of mischief in her eyes. Her father's tirade hadn't affected her one bit. She was getting a new sibling, and nothing was going to spoil her mood. She insisted the child was going to be a girl, and Isaac secretly hoped she was wrong. Every man needed sons, but a better son than Isaac had been to his own father. He had pushed his *daed* away because of the man's strict rules. Rules that had probably kept him safe and grounded throughout his life until Thomas's death.

Levi began to raise a fuss, squirming, his short legs trying to push out of his chair. Mose wiped at the tot's mouth, stood the tiny boy on the floor. The child toddled toward the toy box a few feet away. "That's right. You play while we eat, son. *Mamm*'s busy right now, but she'll be wanting you soon enough."

He looked over at Isaac after wiping down the girls' faces and hands and excusing them from the table. "What could be taking so long? Sarah had Levi so quickly. I was hoping…" His words trailed off. He tugged at his beard as he glanced toward the hallway, then jumped out of his chair as the doorbell chimed. "That'll be *Mamm*. She's come to help Molly deliver the *bobbel*."

Isaac gathered up the dishes, scraping leftovers into the bin. He'd had this job at home as a young boy, his mother believing her sons should know how to fend for themselves in the kitchen as well as her daughters.

Theda hurried into the kitchen, her skirt swinging as she made the sharp turn into the hallway and quickly greeted him. "Hello, Isaac. Forgive me, but I must hurry."

Isaac watched as Otto Fischer patted his son on the back. Mose spoke, his words only for his father's ears. Otto hugged his son, holding on to his hand as he said, "*Ya*, well. This is true, but you should not fret. Sarah will be fine. Greta's death was unfortunate, but not something that happens every day. You know *Gott* is with your *frau*. Soon the *bobbel* will be born. *Gott*'s will be done."

Needing to keep himself busy, Isaac put a kettle of water on to boil and lined up mugs for coffee. It might be a long night, and something hot to drink would soothe the nerves.

"Ah, I thought I heard someone fiddling around in here." Otto stood just inside the kitchen archway, his hat in hand, the gray hair on his head standing to attention from fingers the older man kept running through his disheveled mop. "You're here with Molly?"

"*Ya*, I came to talk to her about the wedding," Isaac said.

"This is a *gut* thing you do, Isaac Graber."

He walked closer and patted him on the back. "Keep your heart open. All this nonsense about lies and Ulla's persistence will pass, and you'll have a fine wife to go home to each night. You mark my words. Molly is a loving woman, but a bit spirited like her *mamm*," he interjected with an amused shrug. "All her life Molly's been a jewel to this community. She can be counted on in a pinch. She'll not disappoint you."

Isaac added a scoop of instant coffee to each cup and stirred, listening to Otto Fischer's words and agreeing with him. He wanted to confess he already had strong feelings for Molly, but didn't say a word. The time wasn't right. Not until she'd heard his story and accepted his past. Until then he would keep words of love to himself.

Drenched in sweat, Sarah writhed on the bed, her body doubled-up in pain. Molly glanced over at the bedside clock. It had been less than two minutes since the birth of the rosy-cheeked baby boy with hair the color of corn. But Sarah still suffered pains as regular as hard labor. Molly had witnessed this situation only once, but felt sure she knew what was happening.

"I feel the need to push again," Sarah cried out, her eyes wild, pleading for help.

Molly and Theda worked as a silent team. The older woman slipped a sliver of ice into Sarah's mouth as Molly pulled back the sheet to do a quick physical examination, and then gasped as a baby shot to the foot of the bed, its tiny body blue and covered in mucus and blood.

Reaching for the soft cloth shoved into the waistband of her apron, Molly gently wiped at the baby girl's mouth and nose, feverishly remembering procedures for underweight babies, facts she'd been taught by her mother. Not bothering to cut the cord yet, she siphoned out what she could from the baby's mouth and then lifted the baby and blew quick, gentle puffs of air into her lungs. Using her finger, Molly cleared the baby's small air passage, blew again and then used her hand to form a funnel for the air to flow through. Molly's heart beat loud in her ears. *Gott, help me. Breathe life into this baby's body.*

"My *bobbel*," Sarah wailed, struggling to sit up. "Is it alive? Please, *Gott*. Let it be alive."

"Don't fret, Sarah. Molly has everything under control. Your *bobbel* will be just fine," Theda promised, her gaze shifting between Sarah and Molly's quick movements.

The blond-haired baby twitched and then moved stronger in Molly's hands, its heart-shaped mouth opening like a tiny bird's as it took in gasps of air and released a whimpering cry. Right before Molly's eyes, the baby's body began to grow pink with life, her cries growing stronger, more robust. "She's alive, Sarah. Your baby girl is alive," Molly sobbed, the stress of the moment taking a toll. "But she's very tiny, maybe four pounds. We should get her to the hospital to be examined by a pediatrician."

Theda rushed to the foot of the bed, assisting as best she could.

Pale and damp with sweat, Sarah's mouth formed a wobbling smile. "Oh, *danke*, *Gott*, *danke*." She fell back against the pillows, weeping softly.

Molly wiped away a tear and waited while Theda tied off the cord in two places, her fingers working nimbly. The surgical knife quickly sliced through the cord, and then Theda swaddled the baby into a soft receiving blanket and placed it into Sarah's waiting arms. "She's a tiny little thing, but her coloring is good," Theda reassured the happy mother. "Keep her against your chest. She needs to stay warm. Molly will call for an ambulance to take you and the *bobbels* to the hospital."

Molly nodded as she wiped off her hands and rushed to the greatroom, her legs flying.

Mose and Isaac looked up as she entered, their excited expressions turning to shock as she babbled, "We'll need an ambulance right away. Sarah's had another baby—a girl—but she's small and needs to be checked out by a doctor."

"But..." Mose stammered, grabbing for his work phone and punching in 911. He glanced over at Isaac and then to his son, cradled in his *daed*'s arms. "Twins? How could she have been pregnant with two and none of us know?"

"Sometimes the smaller baby is behind its larger sibling and its heartbeat isn't heard. The doctor will explain it all soon. I need to get back to Sarah. Hurry, Mose. She and the babies should get to the hospital as soon as possible."

Mose rushed toward the bedroom with Molly as he spoke into the phone, barking the emergency circumstances and his address in Pinecraft.

Isaac stood, his feet rooted to the floor. Molly gave him a grin and patted his cheek before rushing off toward the bedroom.

Locking up the shop, Isaac waved good-night to his new part-time salesman, then turned toward the café, his stomach rumbling. Twinkling Christmas lights beckoned to him from across the dark street.

He dashed between two slow-moving cars and paused at the café door, admiring the beautifully painted nativity scene on the big glass window. Baby Jesus lay in a straw-filled manger, a contented smile on His face…contentment Isaac now shared. He knew life was precious, and Molly saving Mose and Sarah's baby daughter tonight made life seem even more precious. Isaac was proud of her abilities as a midwife, and found himself still smiling as he walked through the café door and searched for an empty spot among noisy *Englisch* and Amish customers.

He glanced around as he shimmied into an empty bench seat, recognizing several familiar families from church. Tomorrow everyone there would know about his engagement to Molly. He sighed, wishing Molly shared the excitement building in him. They were to be married soon, but he knew she still wasn't okay with the plans Otto had laid out for them. He placed his black hat on the café table and ran his hand through his hair.

"What can I get you, Isaac?" Willa Mae appeared next to him, her hands pressed in just above her apron, where her waistline used to be.

He smiled his greeting. "I've never known you to take table orders. Short-staffed tonight?"

Pen poised above a square tablet, Willa Mae grinned a surly smile, showing off her gold-capped front tooth. "Been short-staffed all day. Nothing new in Pinecraft. Employees drop out of sight and don't bother to call in sick. It's the sea. Something strange happens to people when they live close to it. You'll see. Being a shop owner so close to the beach is a hardship." Willa Mae laughed, the sound reverberating through the room, reminding Isaac of the red-suited *Englischer* Santa. "What can I get you?"

"A bowl of your delicious beef stew, if you have any left," Isaac muttered, adding, "with a corn muffin and lots of butter."

"Good choice. The stew's been simmering all day." She scribbled, and her dark eyes glanced at him. "Anything to drink?"

"*Kaffi*, black and strong."

"Kinda late for coffee. You have a bad day?"

He grinned. "Not bad, really, just different. Molly delivered twins, and I was around to see her in action. She's a take-charge kind of woman when it comes to delivering babies."

"That girl's strong-willed and bullheaded, just like her mama."

Isaac frowned, his brow arched in disbelief.

"I'm surprised you'd say she's like her *mamm*. I thought you liked Molly."

Willa Mae squeezed into the empty bench seat across from him, her smile gone as she held his gaze. "Look, I've got no use for Ulla, and never have had, but she's not all bad. Sure she has a mind of her own, but so does Molly." Willa Mae's hands went palms up. "For as long as I've known that little girl, she's been kind and loving, but she has an independent streak as wide as they come. Molly won't admit it—" a smile lit up her face as she spoke Molly's name "—but she's got all her mama's good traits and a few of her bad ones, too. The strong-spirited part she got from Ulla. It's got her in and out of trouble all her life."

Isaac scratched the heavy grizzle on his chin. "She is headstrong, but she's not mean-spirited. Not like Ulla."

She touched him on the arm, her tone quiet. "My old mama taught me not to go judging people. We don't know what motivates that streak of mean in Ulla. Could be she's miserable on the inside, like some old dog with fleas. Misery does strange things to a body. You just be glad Molly doesn't have that mean-spirited part of Ulla's personality." Willa Mae laughed again. "Listen to me spouting off the mouth, taking that old woman's side when she wouldn't give me the time of day. I'll get that stew." Willa Mae cackled as she rose and moved toward the back of the café, greeting her customers and wishing them Merry Christmas as she went.

Thoughts of his run-ins with Molly ran through Isaac's mind. She was headstrong like her *mamm* and determined to stay single. He didn't exactly know what motivated her hesitancy, but perhaps he'd have to rethink his approach toward their upcoming marriage, or lose the independent woman he'd grown to care about. She wouldn't be pushed and might run when she found out about his past.

Racing to get out of the sudden downpour, Molly scrambled through the café's employee entrance, patting rain off her face with the hem of her dress.

Willa Mae poked her head out of the kitchen and laughed at Molly's disheveled appearance. "I told you it was going to rain. My ole joints are never wrong."

"Wish your joints would have told you the rain was coming with high winds and hail the size of olives. I would have gotten a ride home." Her *kapp* slipping to the side, Molly pulled out several pins and repositioned it as she laughed at the silly face Willa Mae pulled.

"Your mama's not right about much, but she's right about one thing. You do have a smart mouth, child."

"I'm sorry. I was just teasing," Molly said with a smile. She prowled the hall wall, searching for the next week's shift list and found it scribbled on the back of a white envelope haphazardly stuck to the wall with a red thumbtack next to several Christmas cards from longtime customers.

Gut, she had Sunday off, but she didn't look forward to church. Otto would be announcing her and Isaac's engagement. She drew in a deep breath, wishing she could be happy about the occasion. She had strong feelings for Isaac, but the idea of trapping him into a marriage he didn't want brought her no joy.

"You have a busy day off?" Willa Mae asked, wiping her damp hands on a dish towel.

"Not really busy, but definitely exciting."

"Here, too." Willa Mae snapped her hairnet back over her ears and washed her hands. "That new girl I hired never showed up for her shift. I been waiting tables like I've got good legs, and you know that's not the case." Willa Mae leaned back and twisted, her spine cracking.

Molly grabbed a clean apron and threw it over her wrinkled dress. "I'll finish her shift and help you clean up at closing."

"You sure? You look beat."

Molly washed her hands next to her boss, her thoughts on what had transpired during the day. "I'm fine, just a little tired from delivering the Fischer babies today."

"Yeah, I heard the good news from Isaac." Willa Mae flipped two sizzling hamburger patties and placed a slice of cheese on both.

"The multiple birth came as a real surprise to us all, but everyone's doing fine now."

"That Fischer woman's gonna have her hands full."

"I know, but she's up to it." Molly quickly rinsed her hands and grabbed a handful of paper towels. "What can I help you with first?"

Willa Mae poked her head out the service window, looked around and then pulled it back in. "Table three needs menus and looks like table five's ready for their second slice of my mama's red velvet cake."

Molly took a quick glance, as well, then pulled back in surprise. Isaac sat in the corner booth, a warm smile lighting up his face as a young girl dressed in a simple pink blouse and jeans leaned across the table and grabbed for an extra napkin. Molly's jaw went slack. "How long has Isaac been talking to her?" Molly whispered, her voice low.

"Not long. Why?"

Molly licked her dry lips. Could this be the girl who had been writing to Isaac? He hadn't said much about his family back in Missouri, but the girl had the same hair coloring and piercing green eyes as Isaac. She could easily be his sister or cousin they looked so much alike.

"He seems to know her pretty good," Willa Mae said, her brow lifting.

"Ya," Molly responded. The young girl spoke, leaning in close. Isaac laughed.

Eyes narrowed, Molly watched as the young brunette brushed back long strands of hair falling across one shoulder. Her youthful giggle floated on the air toward the kitchen.

"Got any idea who she is?" Willa Mae shifted over so Molly could get a better view of what was going on.

"I think so." It was time to find out if this was Rose.

Molly hurried out of the kitchen. She grabbed the coffeepot and headed toward the occupied tables. Two feet from Isaac's booth, she paused and took a deep breath, then casually walked past, her attention on a middle-aged *Englischer* woman with an empty mug.

Three empty mugs later, she headed back toward Isaac and caught him watching her.

"I thought you were off all day," he said in greeting.

She set the coffeepot on an empty table and strolled close. "I was, but Willa Mae needed a hand closing." She looked at the girl across from Isaac and smiled. "Hello, my name's Molly."

"I thought as much. You look just like Isaac described you."

"Molly, this is my little *schweschders*, Rose. She started her *rumspringa* last week and decided to come down on the bus for a quick visit to Pinecraft."

"It's good to meet you," Molly said with a smile, and tugged on her prayer *kapp*. "Seems like you're enjoying your momentary freedom."

"*Ya. Daed* isn't so happy with me traveling alone all this way, but I like to put his teeth on edge. *Mamm* understands my decision to take some time away, so I can decide what I want to do with the rest of my life."

Molly smiled, thinking of her own *rumspringa* and her *daed*'s reaction to her not wearing her prayer *kapp*. "*Daeds* are that way. Always protective of their *kinner* from the *Englischer* world."

Her green eyes sparkling bright, Rose grabbed Molly's hand. "Isaac tells me your banns will be read tomorrow. I'm so happy he's found someone like you after what he went through after Thomas's death."

Molly cut her eyes toward Isaac. Who was Thomas?

Chapter Sixteen

Frazzled after organizing breakfast and dressing Sarah and Mose's three lively, uncooperative children, Molly answered the door.

Theda stood on the porch in the bright sunshine, her reddish hair a riot of uncontrollable curls under her *kapp*. "You look worse for wear, *mein liebling*." She set a plate of iced cupcakes covered in plastic wrap on the small table near the door and put out her arms.

Molly gratefully turned a crying Levi over to his doting *grossmammi*, then picked up the plate of cupcakes. The women headed toward the kitchen.

"*Ya*, I am tired," Molly assured her and then added, "Thank you for bringing these. They'll be a great distraction for Beatrice and Mercy. They keep asking for their *mamm* and new siblings."

Both girls ran to meet their *grossmammi*, accepting kisses and pats on the head with bright smiles.

"I'm sorry to leave you with such a mess in the kitchen," Molly said, the hair around her face and neck damp with sweat. She'd felt so confident when Mose left early that morning for a church meeting. She'd been in charge of the *kinner* before, but today they were uncontrollable. "There just wasn't time to clean up and get the *kinner* dressed, too. I don't know how Sarah manages."

The older woman promptly grabbed a tissue from her pocket, gave Levi's runny nose a swipe, making the *bobbel* fuss even more. She held him on her shoulder and began a soothing back rub. "It's a process, *liebling.*" She raised her voice to be heard over Levi's protests. "Organization is something a mother acquires as she goes along, building her family, one by one. You'll get the hang of it. I promise you."

The image of a tiny boy with Isaac's green eyes and her hair flashed through her mind. She dismissed the thought as foolish. She'd never have children with Isaac. Pretending to be courting the dark-haired man had left her addle-brained and wishing for things she couldn't have. "I hope you're right. I'm sorry to leave you on your own, but I have to hurry." She slipped her shoes on. "I'll be back in a few hours. Are you sure you'll be able to manage these three alone?"

Theda smiled at the two little girls at her feet. "Oh, yes. Beatrice and I have an understanding, don't we, sweet one?" She patted Beatrice on the face. "As long as she behaves, I reward her for good behavior."

Beatrice nodded and smiled at her *grossmammi* and then turned toward the plate of cupcakes on the kitchen table. "I'll be *gut*, but Mercy might be naughty."

They both laughed at Beatrice's statement, but Molly remembered the time and hurried off to change her dress.

Ten minutes later she scurried out of the house, her pink dress flapping behind her as she ran the few blocks to the church. She would be late now, and she'd wanted to be early. She needed to talk with Isaac before services began. They hadn't been able to talk privately the night before with his sister there, but she knew one of them had to talk sense into Otto Fischer soon or their banns would be announced and serious damage done.

Overwarm and out of breath a few minutes

later, Molly stood at the end of the line of young women entering the church's side door.

"You're about to lose your *kapp*," Rachel Lapp, an old school friend and bride-to-be, whispered in Molly's ear. Molly had always envied Rachel. The girl had a sweet, encouraging *mamm*, emotions she had always longed for from Ulla.

Rachel and Ralf Yoder had been an item for years. No one was surprised when they'd announced their wedding plans just before singing practice last October.

Molly scrambled to pull out pins and reposition her prayer *kapp*, her fingers trembling, making the process difficult.

Rachel smiled back at her. "Rumor has it you and Isaac will be announcing your intentions today."

Before she could think, she blurted out, "Who told you?"

With a wink, Rachel smiled. "No one. I just was guessing."

Molly's shoulders fell. She had leaked out her own secret. "*Ya*, well." What could she say to dispel the lie? Nothing, because the lie was fast becoming the truth whether she liked it or not.

Rachel pushed a pin into Molly's *kapp* for

her and fussed with her hair for a moment. "We can't have Isaac seeing you look a mess."

"Danke." She ran her trembling fingers down her prayer *kapp*'s ribbons.

"You seem really nervous, Molly. Maybe you haven't taken enough time to think this engagement through. You've only known Isaac a little while, and courting is such a huge step." Dimples appeared in the girl's cheeks. "Ralf and I dated for two years, but now we can hardly wait to be wed. We've bought a house and started looking at furniture."

Ready to choke on the knot forming in her throat, Molly smiled, hoping her face expressed joy and not the horror she was feeling. "Oh, we're sure. We've done nothing *but* talk about this courtship." Announcing a wedding date, making promises to wed in front of her church family was an important step, and she and Isaac were making a mockery of it. This promise to *Gott* that was meant to be sacred. She had to stop all this somehow.

Isaac glanced around and searched for Molly in the line of worshippers entering the church. He got a fleeting glimpse of Chicken John and Ulla seated several chairs down from him. What were they doing in the engaged-couples row? Molly had mentioned her mother would be getting married, but he'd assumed it was just one of Ulla's stories, something said to upset Molly, who had been close to her father.

Where was Molly? She should have been there by now. He forced himself to sit still and then relaxed as he noticed her standing in a pool of early-morning sunlight just inside the church's side door. She stepped into the building with several other somber-faced young women, a line of school-aged girls following close behind.

Mose waited a few feet away and made a move in Molly's direction. Isaac watched him take her elbow and speak quietly in her ear. She said something to her brother-in-law, her brown eyes animated and sparking fire. She shook her head emphatically. She glanced in Isaac's direction. Her expression told him what he needed to know. She didn't want to join him in the engaged-couples row. Whatever Mose was saying, she was having none of it.

His stomach knotted. Bile threatened another stomachache. Isaac rose but then saw Molly's shoulders droop in surrender. She nodded as Mose spoke again and followed him over to where Isaac stood, her gaze downcast.

Mose greeted Isaac with a firm handshake

and a pat on the back. "I see someone told you where to sit."

"*Ya*, one of the elders." Isaac tried to read Molly's expression as he spoke, but got nothing but a glassy stare from her. She sat on the bench where he'd been sitting. Her back ramrod straight, her hands piously folded in her lap, she looked straight ahead.

"How are Sarah and the *bobbels*?" Isaac asked.

Mose's face lit up at the mention of his wife and babies. His smile was generous. "Oh, they're fine. Just fine. Our little girl is small, but doing fine. The doctor said we owe her life to Molly's expert care. We're so grateful she is a skilled midwife and knew exactly what to do with our surprise *bobbel*." He grinned at Molly, who softened visibly.

Movement at the front of the church had Mose dismissing himself and moving away. He took his place in the line of preachers and deacons who would preach that day.

Molly scooted away, leaving more room than Isaac needed. He tried to catch her gaze as coming church activities were announced at the front of the church, but she stayed focused on the speaker. With a casual twist of her wrist, she dropped her plain white handkerchief to the floor.

Isaac bent to pick up the square white fabric and turned in surprise as Molly bent, too, their heads almost colliding.

"This farce has got to be stopped, Isaac Graber," she whispered, facing him.

"It's too late. Now is not the time—"

"And when *is* the time? After we are tied together with invisible ropes that can't be broken?" Her brown eyes snapped with anger. She straightened, the handkerchief clenched in her fist.

The first song of the morning began. Isaac wanted to sing, but couldn't remember the beautiful song's words, his mind too busy thinking of Molly. She was angry, and he couldn't blame her.

But what could be done about it now?

Two hours later, well-wishers clogged the door of the church. Molly pasted on a smile and pretended to be joyously happy.

"When's the wedding?" an old school friend Molly hadn't seen all winter asked.

"Two weeks, maybe less." She accepted a hug from the animated girl. Molly wanted to be anywhere but here in her home church, telling the good people of Pinecraft she was to marry when she knew every word she spoke was a lie.

A small voice of guilt murmured in her mind. *One lie upon another.* The situation had snowballed out of control, and she had no one to blame but herself.

She accepted another warm embrace from Belinda, a shy girl she'd met and befriended years ago. They'd joined the singing group together, and now both were to be wed. She listened to her friend's words about the food they'd be serving at her wedding, what her special dress was made of.

Molly smiled, but wanted desperately to cry. She had no special dress being made, no house to live with Isaac and no date to announce. Their courtship was nothing but a sham. It took every ounce of strength she had to hold her tongue and not blurt out the truth.

The crowd was thinning, and Molly saw her *mamm* and Chicken John making their way toward them. Her mother grabbed her wrist just as Molly turned away.

"No! Wait, please, Molly," Ulla urged.

Isaac stepped in front of Molly, shielding her. "This is not the time or place for another argument, Ulla. I know you're Molly's *mamm*, but I am to be her husband. I'll have no—"

"Ulla and I have no wish to create chaos, Isaac," Chicken John reassured him. As the bald little man spoke, he kept a white-knuckled grip on his black Sunday hat. "We merely want to wish you both congratulations and a happy life together."

Ulla sniffed, her eyes glistening with tears. She released Molly's wrist and cleared her throat before she spoke, her voice hoarse. "Please give me a moment with *meine dochder*, Isaac. I have things I must say before she weds."

Molly stiffened, ready for the condemnation she knew was coming. Her mother always had an agenda, and this time would be no different.

Isaac glanced at Molly. She gave a curt nod, her stomach heaving. "*Ya*, I will speak with her, but only for a moment." She moved a few feet away. Ulla followed. The two men stood back, waiting.

Her mother's body trembled as she spoke. "*Gott* has been dealing with me harshly for days. I must make my confession known to you." Ulla's chin dropped. "I've been hard on you." The older woman glanced at her husband-to-be. Chicken John smiled his encouragement, his expression hopeful. She looked back to Molly. "John has helped me to see the error of my ways. I have been harsh and often cruel." Her voice broke several times as she continued, "I took my grief out on…you when your *daed* died…and then your sister so soon after."

Ulla took a deep breath and held Molly's gaze, tears sparkling in her eyes. "When Greta died, I died, too. I thought only of myself, of my pain." She began to sob in earnest, her face pinched. "I became bitter and cruel." She took in a shuddering breath. "I am ashamed of my behavior. I gave no regard for your feelings, what you were going through. You were always such a good *kinner*. Kind and respectful."

Ulla grasped Molly's arm again, her fingers cutting into her flesh, her gaze intense, almost desperate. "You've grown into a godly woman, a *dochder* I should be proud of." Ulla swallowed hard. "I need your forgiveness, Molly. Please. Before I go mad with regret."

Molly sidestepped away from her mother, her face warm with threatening tears. Her stomach quivered with nerves. *Could* Mamm *be saying all this to make Chicken John think she's changed?* She desperately wanted to believe her mother had changed for the better.

"Please forgive me, Molly," Ulla urged, taking her hands in hers. Her *mamm*'s chin wobbled as she seemed to search for the right words. "I've been so cruel and demanding. I have no excuse for my selfishness, except that I had a broken heart. I handled things badly and made your life miserable when I should have been comforting you. You lost Greta, too. I'm sorry for all my sins. Please say you forgive me." Tears ran freely down the older woman's wrinkled face as she waited for Molly's response.

Isaac walked forward and slid his arm around Molly's waist. He gave her a gentle squeeze. She glanced up at him, thankful for his bolster of strength.

Trembling, her eyes brimmed with tears. She turned back to face her mother and then slipped her arms around her shoulders. "I forgive you, *Mamm*. No more talk of the past. I have no right to judge." Molly smiled, but her lies ate at her soul. "Today we begin anew as *mamm* and *dochder*."

Chicken John joined them. "*Ya*, this is *gut*, but it makes me to wonder if it's not time to follow the crowd out to the communal meal." He laughed and took Ulla's arm, leading the way to the back of the church.

Isaac tried to take Molly's arm, but she

pulled away from him, making her gesture all about straightening her *kapp*. "*Nee*, it's time to stop the pretense. I'm sick of all the lies."

Chapter Seventeen

Molly stabbed her fork into a tender piece of roast beef and then chewed mechanically. Her thoughts were on the wedding banns Otto Fischer had just declared between herself and Isaac in front of *Gott* and her church family. She'd always thought the banns were sacred, yet here she was squirming in her chair at her own engagement dinner, thinking up ways to get out of the mess she was in.

She glanced over at Isaac, who was sitting next to Chicken John. Both men were eating, wore a smile like everything in the world was perfect. She looked across the table at her *mamm*. Ulla was concentrating on getting the last of her peas on her fork. Her face showed no signs of hidden anger or agenda. Perhaps her *mamm* had meant all she had said. Maybe she was truly sorry for her behavior. For as long as Molly could remember, her mother had never used the word *sorry* in a sentence.

"You're very quiet," Isaac murmured into her ear.

Molly slapped him away like a pesky mosquito. She wanted to talk to him, but not here, not now. "I'm enjoying my meal."

"Then why are you taking such tiny bites?"

She heard a deep rumble of laughter in his chest. How could he enjoy this meal when she was so miserable? "I'm savoring every moment," she muttered back, keeping her eyes on her plate.

Isaac leaned in close to her as he reached for his glass of water. "You're being sarcastic, and it doesn't become you. I need to talk to you. There's so much to explain."

She accepted a slice of pineapple upside-down cake from Helen, Otto's nine-year-old granddaughter, and smiled her thanks. She turned back to Isaac and whispered, "You owe me no explanation. Banns read or not, we are not engaged."

Isaac lifted the chair under him and shoved it over until their chairs touched. "The banns sounded official to me."

To anyone watching they must have looked

like two people very much in love, exchanging sweet words as they ate. "This is not the time to debate the issue, Isaac."

Isaac used his fork to take a bite of her cake, the appreciative sounds he made telling her he liked the cake she'd baked. He had no idea he was eating her secret gift to him, and she wanted it to stay that way, even though it pleased her that he liked the special treat. "We have to talk. You need to know—"

"I'll meet you in the kitchen." She rose and then groaned inwardly as he pushed back his chair, prepared to follow her. "No, not now," she whispered close to his ear. "In a few moments."

Molly scurried across the lawn and into the church kitchen, making her way past women clearing away dishes. When she saw Isaac come in, she motioned him into a quiet corner of the room, away from prying eyes.

He grabbed her arm and pulled her into the broom closet and shut the door behind them. Light bled into the square chamber, casting shadows across Isaac's face. "I haven't had five minutes alone with you for days," he said.

"I know."

They stood toe-to-toe, his height making her feel shorter than her five foot nothing. "I've been busy and so have you." She frowned in frustration and couldn't control her tongue. "Perhaps if you hadn't been avoiding me…"

"I haven't been avoiding you," Isaac shot back. "You didn't seem to want me anywhere near you." Still holding her hand, his thumb brushed back and forth across her fingers. "I didn't know Rose was coming for sure until the day she arrived, or I would have mentioned it sooner."

"I knew she was coming. I saw her letter."

Isaac peered down at her, the dark room making it hard for her to see the expression on his face. "What? How?" he asked.

Conversation could be heard outside the door. She lowered her voice while trying to avoid hitting a row of mop handles with her elbow. "In your room while I was cleaning one day."

His deep, gravely laugh annoyed her. "I never took you for a snoop." He ran his hand up her arm, and she tried to brush it away.

Her face flushed with heat. "I'm not a snoop. I just happened to find the letter on the floor and read the name Rose. I assumed it was from a family member."

"Not a girlfriend? You're so trusting."

"*Ya*, well. But I'm no fool, Isaac Graber. I

know most men have their secrets and can lie at the drop of a hat and be convincing."

"If you'd just listen for a moment, you'd understand so much." Isaac's voice sounded sincere.

"*Ya*, I'll listen, but not here, and only because it will get me away from you and out of this suffocating broom closet."

A half hour later Isaac's feet pushed down hard on the tandem bike's pedals, almost standing in his seat to propel them faster down the road. He tried to adjust for the tipping motion Molly was causing on the second seat. He'd never ridden a two-seater bike before and had no idea it would prove to be so difficult. A strong gust of northerly wind blew across them, and he fought to keep them upright.

"How much farther?"

Molly's words shot past him on the wind. He turned his head slightly, hoping she would be able to hear. "Another block."

"Where exactly did you say we were going?" Molly's voice sounded high-pitched with nerves.

"I didn't say," Isaac told her as he turned into the corner driveway on Lapp Lane. The plain white house looked smaller than he remembered.

The night before he'd come to see the outside of the house with Otto Fischer and been impressed, but in the bright light of day he realized the house was in desperate need of a repair. The peeling exterior was disappointing to say the least. Molly was sure to be dissatisfied and had every right to be, but a home like this was what he could afford for now.

He came to a wobbly stop, his arms and legs braced against the wind. He glanced back to make sure Molly was all right.

"Whose *haus* is this?" Molly asked, her feet slipping from the bike pedals to stand on the stained driveway.

Isaac threw his leg over the bike. "Come inside with me. I have to check some things. It won't take a minute." He waited for her to free her skirt from the bike pedal. With the kick of his boot, he slid the bike stand in place.

"But I thought you said we were going to the park to meet your sister later." Molly straightened her apron and held her *kapp* down with her hand. Strands of hair escaped her bun and danced around her face with another gust of wind.

"*Ya.* We are meeting her, but I have to get this done first. Please come in. I don't want to leave you out on the lawn."

Molly glanced around, her gaze wandering to the peeling front porch swing swaying in the breeze. "Who lives here?"

Isaac took the crook of her arm and led her toward the house. "No one, right now."

She hesitated, pulling back. "Then why are we here?"

"Otto sent me on a mission. I have to check out the work needing to be done on the inside."

"Oh."

At the door he patted his pants pockets until he found the key ring and then dug it out, along with a piece of chewing gum and three dimes. The lock fought the key. He turned it upside down and the key slid in, the door creaking as it opened.

Isaac used his hand to push the door open all the way and then flip up the light switch. Nothing. No electricity. He stepped inside. Molly trailed silently behind him.

Bright sunlight flooded the small entry hall. The inside of the house appeared dingy, the walls needing a wipe down and thick coat of paint. They moved into the greatroom. All the blinds and curtains were drawn, leaving the space in gloom. Dust particles floated on the midday sun streaming in through the opened door behind them.

"It needs some work," Isaac commented.

Molly nodded in agreement. "*Ya*. A lot of work."

"Let's get some light in here."

Molly went with Isaac to the windows. She pushed against the drab olive-green drapes at the double window and shoved them open.

Isaac jerked on the cord behind the folds of curtain fabric and stepped back to avoid the avalanche of dust swirling around them.

Silently, both turned back to the room.

A huge peace sign had been spray-painted in black on the white back wall, just behind a mud-colored couch that had seen better days.

"Not good."

"*Nee*." Isaac's heart sank as he watched Molly inspect the room, her head shaking in distaste.

She pinched off a dust cover with two fingers and revealed a sturdy tan recliner that rocked gently back and forth. Molly smiled at her discovery. "At least the chair looks usable," she murmured, and headed for the open kitchen off the big room. "*Ya*, well. Come look at this, Isaac."

He ambled over, noticing missing light fixtures, and several holes in the wall the size of a fist. The ceramic tile underfoot appeared dingy, but none seemed cracked. He rounded the corner and entered the kitchen.

His breath caught as he took in missing drawers and a hole in the counter where the sink had been. "At least they left the faucet." He tried to sound positive, but heard disappointment laced in his words.

"Ya." She pulled open the oven door and gasped. "What kind of people lived here?" Years of cooking had left the inside of the range the color of rust. She shut the door and moved away. The odor of burned-on food followed them across the room.

"Let's check out the bedrooms and then get out of here." Isaac led her down a dim hallway. He peeked into the decent-sized bathroom and promptly shut the door. "Lots of work to do in there." He knew the room would need gutting, the black-ringed, moldy tub scarred and unsalvageable.

The back bedrooms proved less depressing. They needed a coat of paint and the closet doors needed to be rehung, but nothing too drastic.

"This must be the master bedroom," Molly said, ambling over to the bare window. "The view from here is lovely. Look at those rosebushes against the fence. All they need is a good pruning. The lawn can be reseeded and watered. There could be red roses blooming and grass to mow by spring."

Isaac walked up behind her and put his hand on the windowsill. "What do you think of the *haus*, Molly? Does it have promise?"

"Promise?" Molly turned to him, something in her gaze giving him hope. "*Ya*, it has promise. All it needs is a few repairs and lots of paint and love. The bones are sound. I like the view from this window a lot. If it were my house…" She stopped speaking and looked up at him, a spark in her eyes telling him she was on to him. "Why did you bring me here, Isaac? This isn't a project for Otto, is it?"

"*Ya*, it is Otto's *haus*. He bought it as a rental a few days ago, but it could be our home once it's fixed up, if you'd let it be."

"What do you mean, *our* home? I thought—"

Isaac took her arm and pulled her close. "I feel different now. I'm all for us getting married, starting a family here in Pinecraft…if that's something you could live with."

He tried to hold her gaze, but she looked away, hiding her true feelings from him. "You lied to back me up, to protect me from my *mamm*'s plans for a loveless marriage. You had no interest in a wife. I remember you saying you couldn't afford one because the shop wasn't doing that well." She looked up at him, her gaze somber and searching.

"*Ya*, I did say that, but only at first. Before I…" Isaac knew now was the time to declare his love, but the tender words scrambled in his mind and wouldn't come off his tongue. How did a man tell a woman that she meant more to him than the very breath he drew and then confess himself to be a murderer?

"Before what? You can't be talking about love."

He drew air into his lungs and began to speak, praying his words were the right ones to convince her how much she meant to him. "I wanted to tell you for weeks that my feelings have changed, but there was so little time. There's so much you don't know about me, about my past."

Molly's brown eyes blinked back glistening tears, her chin trembling. "But you never said the words *I love you.*"

Isaac's shoulders slumped, the weight of his own stupidity oppressing him. He looked down at the dirty floor underfoot. *What must she think, listening to my ramblings?* "I do love you and would have told you sooner, but I thought if I told you the truth about my past, you wouldn't want me in your life. I behaved like the coward I am."

"You're no coward, Isaac. You're the man I love. Please tell me about your past. All of it."

Isaac's lips brushed hers in a gentle kiss and then his words came fast, his deep voice quivering with emotions he'd held back for too long. "Like here in Pinecraft, the teens from Amish and Mennonite churches back home get together and play volleyball on Saturday afternoons in the summertime. A few months ago my friend Thomas twisted his ankle while playing, and since we lived close to each other, I offered to drive him the two miles to his *daed's* farm."

With a trembling hand, Isaac rubbed away a tear rolling down his cheek. "I'd driven his old truck before, but never on the country roads." His gaze caught hers, and he almost smiled. "You know how farm boys behave. We'd take turns driving around the freshly plowed fields like young fools."

Molly nodded, her eyes searching his.

"It had gotten dark, and Thomas was lying in the back of the truck so he wouldn't hurt his ankle." Pools of tears filled Isaac's eyes, making them red. "We were almost to his home when the accident happened." Big tears rolled down his cheeks, one after another.

He took Molly's hands and squeezed hard. "I tried to get out of the way of the other vehicle. I fought the wheel, but the lights kept coming straight at us."

He stopped talking, as if his mind were exploding with memories. A sob escaped his lips. "I must have been knocked out. When I came to, Thomas lay on the ground near me, but I couldn't go to him." He slapped his thigh. "My leg was a mess, but I called out to him. Begged him to be all right." He gulped in air, his breathing fast and hard. "It only took a few minutes for the *Englischer* police officer to show up, but it seemed forever. I must have passed out again because when I woke up I saw Thomas's body being placed on a stretcher."

Isaac stared into his memories, his eyes glassy. "I knew he was dead. He wasn't moving, and there was blood all over." He took in a deep breath. "Later at the hospital, the police told me the accident wasn't my fault. That the drunk driver of the other vehicle was to blame, but I knew better. I killed Thomas that day. I was driving the truck. It was my lack of experience that killed him. My *daed* wouldn't let me confess to the police. He said we Amish care for our own, but I wanted to tell the truth, take the blame for what I had done, no matter what the *Englischer* police would do to me." Deeps sobs escaped Isaac as she gathered him in her arms and cried with him in pain and regret.

Chapter Eighteen

The next day Liesel Troyer, Molly's friend, yelled from the sidelines of the shuffleboard court. "Knock her out of there!"

Molly bent, estimated wind and distance, eyed the round yellow disk and then propelled her puck down the court. It hit Rose's disk with a loud whack, sending it flying to the side.

Too competitive for her own good, Molly held her breath as she continued to watch the trajectory of the disk. It slowed to a crawl and then came to a stop exactly where she'd planned. *I've won!*

Rose sprang off the bench and good-naturedly hugged Molly's neck, her loose, *Englischer* styled hair blowing in the wind as they congratulated each other on the entertaining game of shuffleboard.

"I'm so glad you came to Pinecraft," Molly said with a grin, taking in Rose's sweet smile, the sparkle in her dark green eyes. At first she'd dreaded meeting Rose, but she'd been wrong to worry. The dark-haired girl, who looked so much like Isaac, turned out to be a charmer, high-spirited, with a winning personality everyone seemed to love. Molly felt sure Rose would grow into a sister and not an enemy as she feared.

"Me, too," Rose shouted over the noise of the shuffleboard players, her smile as genuine as a child's.

Molly searched for Isaac in the sea of faces around them and found him nodding, deep in conversation with Otto and Mose Fischer, at a domino table. She grinned, his words of love the day before still ringing in her ears, warming her heart. She was still reeling from his painful story of Thomas's death. No wonder Isaac had seemed so miserable when he'd first arrived in Pinecraft. His guilt had been eating at him, destroying his sanity. She smiled again as he looked up and caught her watching him. Her love for him grew stronger with each passing hour.

"You think we should disturb them?" Molly asked, sliding her arm through Rose's as they pushed their way through the crowd of Amish and Mennonite vacationers.

"Absolutely. I'm starving," Rose said, and took the lead. "Excuse me. Pardon," she muttered as she buffeted people, her smile never fading.

Otto rose and motioned them over, his disapproving gaze flicking over Rose's jeans and frilly blouse of bright red fabric. "So this is your sister, Rose," he said to Isaac.

Rose put out her hand, her smile widening, displaying perfect white teeth.

Otto took the hand she offered and returned her smile. "Hello, Rose," he said and turned to Mose. "This is my son, Mose. He's our local furniture builder and church elder."

Mose shook the young woman's hand, his expression friendly, "*Willkumm* to Pinecraft. Isaac tells me you've just started your *rumspringa*."

Rose laughed. "*Ya*. I thought I'd visit my brother before going back home and coming to terms with my faith."

"If we can give you any assistance in making your decision, come and see me and Sarah. Isaac knows our address," Mose offered.

"We thought we'd go get something to eat. I'm starving." Rose pulled on Isaac's arm, urging him out of his chair.

"Rose is always hungry. She has my appetite." Isaac smiled at his sister, who grimaced at him but didn't deny his accusation.

Mose rose. "Why don't all of you come back to the house with Molly? Marta and Kurt, my brother and sister-in-law, are in town, helping out with the babies now that Sarah's finally home. Marta made a huge pot of chicken and dumplings this morning and chocolate whoopie pies were cooling on racks when I left. I'm sure there's more than enough for everyone. Besides, Sarah will want the chance to show off the *bobbels*."

Molly watched Theda Fischer's shoulders sway as she comforted her whimpering *gross-dochder* with a gentle back rub, her blue-eyed gaze on the sleeping twin who lay tightly swaddled in a blue blanket a few feet away in his tiny cot. She tucked in the little girl's pink arm and adjusted the baby's blanket before she turned to her son, Mose, who sat next to her. "It makes me to wonder if the New Year will be rung in long before these *bobbels* get a name."

Sarah and Mose exchanged a knowing glance across the table. "We have named them, but only this morning," Sarah admitted. "They are to be Wilhelm and Rebecca, or Willie and

Becka, as Beatrice called them before she left for Ulla's *haus*." Sarah grinned at Theda's joyous expression. "Beatrice says *Gott* spoke to her in a dream about the names, but I think this time she just wanted to honor her *great-gross-mammi* and *great-grossdaadi*, as Mose did when he named Beatrice after Ulla's mother."

Theda grinned. "My *mamm* and *daed* would have been so pleased. They were good people, full of *Gott*'s love. To name the *bobbels* after them is such a special blessing. *Danke*, both of you."

"It is our pleasure, *Mamm*. Sarah loves you as much as I do and was happy to honor your parents. You are the *mamm* Sarah never had and for that I am grateful."

Molly ate the last bite of her chicken and dumplings, contentment putting a perpetual smile on her face. She had a future with Isaac and had accepted his love. Nothing, not even the death of Thomas, could spoil her joy.

Her gaze drifted across the table to where Isaac sat in a chair next to Rose. He reached over and patted his sister's hand as he said, "It's been such a pleasure eating with this wonderful family. I've missed these kind of meals, where love is shared in abundance."

Rose turned to Isaac and added, "Like our

meals at home. I've missed *Mamm* and *Daed*. It's been a week since I've seen them."

Otto laid down his napkin and cleared his voice with the authority of a judge. "Perhaps it is time to consider your options, Rose. Is the *Englischer* life for you, or will you be baptized and become a part of your community?"

Rose grinned and said, "You'll be glad to know I've decided to go home and join the church."

An hour later Sarah was feeding tiny Rebecca. "This child is never full." Sarah laughed, her finger trailing down her newest daughter's rosy cheek. The child turned toward its mother's finger and tried to suckle.

"Her hair is darker than Levi's, almost a honey color," Rose commented, her arms filled with baby Wilhelm, who was twice the size of his diminutive sister.

Molly sat in a chair by the window, enjoying the evening breeze and the close family interaction, but her mind soon wandered to Christmas next year. Would she be the one holding a *bobbel*, a child with her brown eyes and Isaac's good looks and dark hair?

"You're very far away, Molly. Something bothering you, or is it the wedding coming up in a matter of days?" Sarah bent to change Rebecca's mini-sized diaper.

Twisting, Molly faced her mentor and friend. "*Nee*. I wasn't thinking about the wedding, although I must, and soon. Time is flying."

Sarah placed her freshly diapered daughter into Theda's eager arms and strolled over to her bedroom closet, motioning with her finger for Molly to follow her. "Come with me. I have something to show you." She smiled, revealing a mischievous side to Sarah that Molly hadn't seen before. The mother of five turned on the light in a deep closet big enough to be a bedroom and went directly to a large plastic bag hanging among simple Amish dresses in every shade of the rainbow.

Sarah pulled off the protective plastic bag. A shimmery *kapp*, delicately fashioned out of the finest woven linen and lined with satin threads hung from a padded hanger. Behind it another hanger held a pale pink dress of polished cotton, the cut simple but beautifully stitched.

"Oh, Sarah. What a beautiful dress. Is this what you're wearing for Christmas?" Molly fingered the soft fabric of the skirt, touched the tiny flowers embroidered along the neckline.

Sarah tucked her arm around Molly's waist and smiled down at her, the dress held high off the floor. "*Nee*, silly goose. This dress is for your wedding day."

"*Mein* dress?" Overwhelmed with joy, Molly took the garment and pressed it to her chest. "Oh, look. It's the correct length. How did you guess so perfectly?"

Sarah laughed. "I didn't guess. I snuck one of your dresses out of your closet and took measurements for the ladies in the sewing circle who made the dress in just two days. It should fit perfectly."

"*Ya*, it should." Molly grinned at herself in the mirror, her surprise showing in her expression. "But how did you know for sure Isaac and I would marry? I wasn't sure myself."

"I had a feeling," Sarah said, smiling.

Molly smiled back. "*Gott* must approve of this marriage. He has been so faithful and made a way for all this to happen."

Sarah nodded. "Mose told me Otto has found a *haus* for you two. That should relieve your mind some."

"It did. We'll be renting the fixer-upper. *Gott* bless Otto Fischer. He's always there for me when I need him, just like Mose. The house will become a wonderful home once the work is completed." Molly worried her *kapp* ribbons, her mind revisiting the abandoned house, the long list of repairs that needed doing. Would it be ready in time?

"I heard the men talking around the table earlier this morning. Seems Isaac hired a man to work a full week at the bike shop, so he's free to gut the bathroom and kitchen. Mose and Otto will be putting in all new fixtures, a new sink and counters in the kitchen. Several men from the church will be painting once the dust settles. I don't think you have anything to worry about. I can't wait to see the house so I can make drapes for you and maybe a quilt for the new bed."

Theda slipped into the clothes-filled room, Rebecca asleep in her arms. "Oh, Sarah. You and the ladies have outdone yourselves. That dress came out beautiful!"

Rose quickly followed Theda in and caught her breath as she viewed the dress and *kapp* up close. "Molly, what a lucky girl you are. I am *so* impressed. You'll make such a beautiful bride. My brother will fall over his own big feet when he sees you in this."

Molly erupted into giggles, picturing Isaac saying his vows from the floor at her feet. "He may be a bit of a klutz, but he's a wonderful klutz and I love him more than I can say."

Chapter Nineteen

The Florida sun blazed outside, the December day perfect for a wedding.

Sarah's large bedroom was full of women, some ready to assist Molly as she dressed, while others seemed content to sit around, laughing aloud at the silly things Rose was sharing about Isaac as a boy.

"I kid you not, Molly. Isaac was impossible to live with between the ages of ten and fourteen. He was constantly in trouble with *Daed*, either for stealing the buggy and taking all his friends on joyrides, or coming home late and missing his ten o'clock curfew."

Molly smiled at the picture Rose painted. She would have loved to have known the rambunctious, mischievous Isaac, the man he'd been before Thomas's tragic death. *Gott* willing, he'd return to that same happy man with time and healing.

She was glad to see Rose had changed out of the jeans and a comical kitten T-shirt she'd worn at breakfast, into a plain dress in pale yellow, fit for an Amish wedding. She still wore no *kapp*. Her shiny dark hair curled around her shoulders, free from the traditional constraints of the bun most Amish women wore.

Otto would throw a fit when he saw her, but Molly knew nothing would be said in public. The wise old man understood *rumspringa* sometimes sent *youngies* into a spin, their decision to join the church, or not, often stymied their decision making for months, sometimes years. Rose was settling down, and once she was back in Missouri Molly felt sure Rose would join the church and find her way her way back to her Amish roots.

Her heart beat fast in her ears as Sarah breezed out of the closet and brought out the wedding dress. A hush fell over the room and then a united clap of hands broke out as the beautifully made dress was lifted over Molly's head and slid into place.

Two hours later, Molly stepped over the threshold of her and Isaac's new home. She

laughed when she saw the banner over the fire-
place that read ISAAC AND MOLLY GRA-
BER.

"Did you know about this?" she asked her
new husband, her gaze flitting around the perfect room. A traditional vase of flowering celery stalks decorated the beautiful dining room
table in the alcove.

"I had no idea, but you know my sister was
probably the ringleader of all this hoopla,"
Isaac said with a grin.

"Your sister does have a flair for the dra-
matic," Molly said with a laugh, sitting on the
plush tan couch, another piece of furniture
she'd never seen before. "Where did all this
furniture come from? I thought we'd be sitting on crates and saving every penny we could
spare for furniture."

"*Nee*. Otto wouldn't hear of you doing without. He and Theda made it happen. So many
people from the community donated to our
cause and kept it a secret. Even Willa Mae."

"Willa Mae kept a secret? I'm shocked. She's
usually the first to spill the beans. She never
said a word all week. Wait till I see her." Molly
laughed good-naturedly and hugged Isaac
close. She took in all the changes to the kitchen
behind them. "You've been busy in there. Look

at this place. It's much too fancy for us. Granite countertops?"

Minutes later, hand in hand, Isaac trailed behind Molly as she made her way to the back of the house. "Oh, look. We do have a bathroom, and a wonderful one at that." The new white sink, toilet and tub sparkled in the filtered sunlight shining in through an oblong window over the tub.

Setting on the counter, a bowl of homemade soap balls filled the room with the fragrance of roses. "I see Rose was in here, too," Molly remarked with a grin, and touched a fluffy hanging towel in a pale shade of blue.

"Can you tell blue is Rose's favorite color?" Isaac asked, and smiled at Molly's reflection in the mirror.

Molly had experienced joy many times in her life, but no emotion had prepared her for the feeling of contentment she felt rushing through her. She grabbed Isaac's hand and hurried him down the hall, her excitement almost more than she could contain. "I can't wait to see our bedroom."

She opened the door slowly and gasped with surprise. The room looked like a picture from a fancy *Englischer* magazine, the bed neatly made and covered in the most beautiful wedding-ring-patterned quilt she'd ever seen. Sarah's work, no doubt. Two dark wooden nightstands flanked the bed, with matching lamps placed on each. Across the room a tallboy dresser, with six big drawers, graced the wall. "This is all too much," Molly whispered and sat on the bed, tears blurring her vision. "I thought—"

"I know." Isaac sat beside her, slid his arm around her shoulders. "You thought you were coming home to a fixer-upper and a list of must-haves a mile long."

"*Ya*—" her chin wobbled "—I did, but just look at all this." She spread her hands wide-open and then wiped away a tear.

Isaac laughed out loud, his voice deep and rumbling. "You make me so happy, Molly."

She leaned in close and pressed her head to his chest, listening to the steady beat of his heart. "And you, my love, are my joy. My everything."

His hands were gentle as he pulled her close. He lowered his lips to hers, and just before they touched, he whispered, "And you are mine."

* * * * *

Dear Reader,

Thank you for choosing to read *The Amish Midwife's Courtship*. It was a joy to return to Pinecraft, Florida, the tiny Amish tourist town just outside of Sarasota and to introduce you to spirted Molly Ziegler, as she intertwined her life with guilt-ridden Isaac Graber.

I hope you enjoyed getting reacquainting with the community's wise old bishop, Otto Fischer, and with spirited widow Ulla Ziegler, who insisted she be put in this book, too (that woman kept me up nights wondering what she'd get up to next). I gave you a quick glance back at Mose and Sarah Fischer and their sweet children, Beatrice and Mercy, the family who made my first Pinecraft book, *The Amish Widow's Secret*, such fun to write.

It's always good to hear from my readers. You can contact me at cheryl.williford@att.net for a chat.

May God richly bless you and bring you peace,

Cheryl Williford

LARGER-PRINT BOOKS!

GET 2 FREE
LARGER-PRINT NOVELS
PLUS 2 FREE
MYSTERY GIFTS

Love Inspired®

SUSPENSE
RIVETING INSPIRATIONAL ROMANCE

Larger-print novels are now available...

REQUEST YOUR FREE BOOKS!
2 FREE WHOLESOME ROMANCE NOVELS IN LARGER PRINT
PLUS 2
FREE
MYSTERY GIFTS

✫✫✫✫✫✫✫✫✫✫✫✫✫✫✫✫✫✫✫✫✫✫✫✫

HEARTWARMING™

✾✾✾✾✾✾✾✾✾✾✾✾✾✾✾✾✾✾✾✾✾✾✾✾

Wholesome, tender romances

YES! Please send me 2 FREE Harlequin® Heartwarming Larger-Print novels and my 2 FREE mystery gifts (gifts worth about $10). After receiving them, if I don't wish to receive any more books, I can return the shipping statement marked "cancel." If I don't cancel, I will receive 4 brand-new larger-print novels every month and be billed just $5.24 per book in the U.S. or $5.99 per book in Canada. That's a savings of at least 19% off the cover price. It's quite a bargain! Shipping and handling is just 50¢ per book in the U.S. and 75¢ per book in Canada.* I understand that accepting the 2 free books and gifts places me under no obligation to buy anything. I can always return a shipment and cancel at any time. Even if I never buy another book, the two free books and gifts are mine to keep forever.

161/361 IDN GHX2

Name	(PLEASE PRINT)	

Address		Apt. #

City	State/Prov.	Zip/Postal Code

Signature (if under 18, a parent or guardian must sign)

Mail to the **Reader Service:**
IN U.S.A.: P.O. Box 1867, Buffalo, NY 14240-1867
IN CANADA: P.O. Box 609, Fort Erie, Ontario L2A 5X3

* Terms and prices subject to change without notice. Prices do not include applicable taxes. Sales tax applicable in N.Y. Canadian residents will be charged applicable taxes. Offer not valid in Quebec. This offer is limited to one order per household. Not valid for current subscribers to Harlequin Heartwarming larger-print books. All orders subject to credit approval. Credit or debit balances in a customer's account(s) may be offset by any other outstanding balance owed by or to the customer. Please allow 4 to 6 weeks for delivery. Offer available while quantities last.

Your Privacy—The Reader Service is committed to protecting your privacy. Our Privacy Policy is available online at www.ReaderService.com or upon request from the Reader Service.

We make a portion of our mailing list available to reputable third parties that offer products we believe may interest you. If you prefer that we not exchange your name with third parties, or if you wish to clarify or modify your communication preferences, please visit us at www.ReaderService.com/consumerschoice or write to us at Reader Service Preference Service, P.O. Box 9062, Buffalo, NY 14240-9062. Include your complete name and address.

HW15

READERSERVICE.COM

Manage your account online!

- Review your order history
- Manage your payments
- Update your address

> *We've designed the*
> *Reader Service website*
> *just for you.*

Enjoy all the features!

- Discover new series available to you, and read excerpts from any series.
- Respond to mailings and special monthly offers.
- Connect with favorite authors at the blog.
- Browse the Bonus Bucks catalog and online-only exculsives.
- Share your feedback.

Visit us at:

ReaderService.com